FEAR INC.

VOLUME 3

MELINDA VALENTINE

LIMITLESS PUBLISHING, LLC

Fear Inc: Volume 3

Copyright © 2022 by Melinda Valentine.

All rights reserved.

First Print Edition: December 2022

Limitless Publishing, LLC

Kailua, HI 96734

www.limitlesspublishing.com

Formatting: Limitless Publishing

ISBN-13: 978-1-64034-651-2

DEDICATION

Readers… This one is for you

ACKNOWLEDGMENTS

Let me start by thanking all of you, the readers. You've waited a long time for Kasper to get his HEA. I'm forever grateful for all your support.

Thank you, Limitless Publishing, for taking a chance on an unknown author six years ago.

My kids, you will always be my greatest success.

My husband, RJ. They don't make 'em like you anymore. I'm so glad you're mine.

Thank you all from the bottom of my heart. Much love.

PROLOGUE

Six Years Ago

KRYSTA ROLLED over onto her side, resting her head on her perched hand, to get a better view of Kasper as he stood by the cliff's edge overlooking their little town. He was gorgeous. The moonlight caressed his bare shoulders and back from this angle. The soft breeze tousled his hair. It was longer than it was when they started seeing each other six months ago. Now it would actually stay behind his ear and curl around the lobe when he pushed it there.

She never tired of looking at him. She knew if he'd asked her, she would gladly look her fill for the rest of her life. She sat up, rummaging around their blankets for her clothes. She stood up, slipping her feet into her panties before pulling her jeans on. Once her bra and shirt were back on, she wrapped her arms around him from behind. He crossed his arms around hers, holding her to him.

"Hey there, Kitten. It's getting late. As much as I don't want to, I better get you home."

He turned to face her, a big goofy smile on his lips.

Krysta stretched up on her tip-toes, pressing a kiss to them. It was soft and sweet. Nothing like the heated wet kisses of earlier, yet no less mesmerizing.

"You're so unbelievably beautiful." He pressed his lips to hers again.

Kissing Kasper had been a fantasy for longer than she cared to admit even to herself. Now, she could indulge whenever her heart desired. Well, not really, they were still hiding their relationship from everyone. That was why she needed to woman up. They wouldn't be able to hide much longer. She'd been nervous all night. She had to tell him. This moment. In their place, was perfect.

"Before we go, I have something to tell you."

"You can tell me anything." He grinned down at her, clasping his hands at the small of her back. "What dirty little fantasy are you cooking up now?"

I wouldn't call it a dirty fantasy. Perhaps scandalous. She sucked in a large breath, slowly blowing it out.

"I'm pregnant." She smiled up at him. There she said it. Now it suddenly felt real. As if sharing the news with him made it real and not just a notion. She had loved Kasper for so long, even though she wasn't ready now, she would get there. She had seven months to prepare. There wasn't anyone else she would want to do this with. Kasper was it for her. She knew it like she knew her own name.

The smile she so dearly loved slowly slipped from his face. "Are you playin' with me?"

"Of course not. Who would do such a thing?"

"You're pregnant?"

"Yes." She couldn't understand why he was looking at her that way.

He let go of her and took a step back. "Is it mine?"

"Is it..." She felt as though he'd smacked her in the

2

face. It would have hurt a lot less if he had. "You're the only one I've ever been with, and you fucking know it, Kass."

He ran his fingers through his hair, refusing to make eye contact. She touched his arm, only to have him pull away. She understood it was probably a shock. Hell, it was to her too when she found out. When the package says ninety-nine percent effective, you never think you'll be the one percent. Lucky her. Kasper pulled his shirt back on, then picked up their blanket.

"Kasper, talk to me," she pleaded.

"If we don't leave now, you'll miss curfew."

He left her standing there alone as he started down the footpath. Krysta could either follow or get left out here. She scurried after him. She could hear his Harley roar to life before she even cleared the tree line. His head was lowered as he held out her helmet. She slipped it on her head before swinging her leg over the bike. At least he waited for her to wrap her arms around him before he took off. The ride back to town was tense. He didn't squeeze her hands or reach back to rub her thigh while her drove like he usually did.

Krysta couldn't help the sinking feeling in her stomach. The one saying this was the last ride she would take with her arms wrapped around the man she desperately loved. Kasper stopped his bike at the end of her street like always. Kasper thought it would be better to see how things went before they broke the news to Paxton. He didn't want to lose his best friend and Krysta didn't want her brother to worry if it ended up being just a fling.

For her, it wasn't a fling. Every molecule of her being was madly in love with Kasper Guttenmuth.

She couldn't bring herself to get off the bike. Now that

she thought about it, it would be the last time she'd ride behind him, holding him tight. No matter what happened between them, it wasn't safe for her. She couldn't risk anything happening to the baby now. He felt stiff under her arms, his hands remaining on the handlebars. Slowly she dismounted.

"Kasper," she whispered.

"I'm sorry I said that. I know you haven't been with anyone else."

Relief flooded through her. Maybe he just needed some time. It took her a whole week to tell him.

"Don't worry. I'll pay for it," he said while tucking her helmet into his saddlebag.

"Pay for what?"

"The abortion. It's my responsibility."

For the second time tonight Krysta felt her world tip. Abortion. How could he even suggest that? She'd mentioned a few times, in the last six months alone, her feelings on that topic. She was pro-choice, but her choice was no. She would rather raise this baby on her own. She really hoped she wouldn't have to.

She straightened her shoulders, holding her head high. "I'm not doing that. I'm having this baby."

"Damn it, Krysta. This wasn't supposed to happen."

"Maybe we didn't plan it, but it did happen."

"I'm not the fathering type."

"Obviously, you are."

"I can't be someone's father, Krysta. Not now, maybe not ever."

Krysta felt her heart splintering into a million pieces. She pressed her shaking hands to her stomach as nausea rolled through her. She wasn't sure if it was from the realization she was going to be raising this baby on her own after all, or if morning sickness was once again rearing its ugly head. Unable to breathe through it, she turned quickly to the hedges behind her to vomit.

"Are you gonna be okay to walk home?"

The burning in her throat lit a fuse to ignite a fire in her belly. He didn't get to see her vulnerable ever again. Her father's words echoed in her ear. *"A man worthy of your love, baby girl, will always show you what you mean to him. Don't listen for flowery words. He may not know how to speak to them, but he will always show you if you're paying attention."*

Straightening, she wiped her mouth on the sleeve of her sweatshirt. Kasper still straddled his bike. She'd hoped she would see regret or pain in his eyes. Something to show her what he felt for her. Nothing. That's what she saw looking back at her. A blank mask devoid of any emotion, good, bad, or indifferent. This was it. It was time for her to walk away. Time to go back to pretending she wasn't in love with the man before her. She'd had to do just that for years. She could do it again. Fake it till you make it, they say.

"You don't need to worry about me anymore, Kasper." Without waiting for him to reply, she started walking down the dark street to her house. Alone.

ONE
KRYSTA

Present Day

KRYSTA GRIPPED her Ruger with shaky hands. Creeping through the back door, she moved quickly but quietly past the kitchen and living room. She found the staircase going upstairs. One foot in front of the other, as close to the wall as she could get to lessen the chance of a creaky floorboard, she ascended to the upper floor. She could hear voices but couldn't make out the words. The door was open at the end of the hall. A soft glow beckoned her. She switched the gun to the other hand, wiping her sweaty hand down her jeans before adjusting her right-handed grip yet again.

Moving down the hallway, Krysta clicked the safety off. Without hesitation, she rushed into the room only to find she was too late. Cori lay lifeless in a pool of her own blood, unseeing eyes staring up at the ceiling. Paxton was tied to a chair to her right. The anguish in his eyes almost brought her to her knees. The man standing behind him drew his knife high above his head before plunging it into her brother's chest.

Krysta woke up screaming, her body slick with sweat. She brushed her wet, matted hair from her face with the crook of her arm, her dream slowly fading as she reacquainted herself with her surroundings. She lifted herself onto her elbows, letting her eyes adjust to the dark. Bentley lay sound asleep next to her, a sleep mask covering his eyes and plugs filling his ears. He'd stopped waking up with her after the first few weeks of her reoccurring nightmares. He said he needed his rest—like she didn't.

They were frequent still after all these months. Sometimes they played out like a memory. Other nights, like tonight, she was too late, her mind playing out what might have been. Taking a deep breath, she gave in. There was no sense lying there wide awake. There would be no more sleep tonight. Slithering out of bed, she snatched Bentley's button-down shirt off the edge of the mattress. Slipping it on her shoulders, she continued fastening the buttons on the way to the kitchen.

Her hands shook slightly as she poured herself a glass of orange juice. The light from the open fridge cast shadows throughout the room. She was sick and tired of the dreams that haunted her. They replayed the image of her taking another man's life. Repeatedly. She knew without a doubt, given the same situation, she would have done it all over again. She'd saved Cori's life and her brother's. That man wouldn't have stopped once he'd killed Cori. He would have had no choice except to silence Paxton too.

Cori had moved in next door to her brother a few months earlier. Sparks flew immediately between the two of them. They were perfect for each other. Her stubborn ass brother almost screwed it all up, thankfully he came to his senses, and now Cori was living with him. She was incredibly happy for them both.

She wanted to call her big brother, but it was the middle of the night. She didn't want to wake him or Cori. He worried about her enough as it was. She carried her juice and a banana to the kitchen table and sat down. Opening her laptop, she continued to work on a project she was already two weeks ahead of schedule on. At this rate she would be done in a day or two. The client would certainly be happy.

She loved her job as a freelance graphic designer. She was able to take on as many jobs and clients as she wished and work as many hours as she wanted as long as she finished by the deadline. Plus, she could work from anywhere in the world that had a Wi-Fi connection. If she wanted to work on a beach in Maui, there was nothing stopping her.

She was contemplating laying back down for a few hours when Bentley waltzed into the kitchen. He'd showered and was dressed in a black designer suit. A white shirt and navy tie completed the look. He was a good-looking man. He had a toned, lean body, but not bulging with muscles. He had a stunning smile and was super smart. His father was a well-known politician. Although he hadn't come right out and said anything, Krysta knew he had similar aspirations in the future. She liked spending time with him. He treated her nice and they never fought. At least they hadn't in the past. Since the night she saved Cori's life, things had been different. They still didn't fight, but that was probably because Bentley refused to continue what he thought was an unpleasant conversation. If she pushed, he simply left the room.

After a few months they were already living in a routine. They never did anything spontaneous. The only time he surprised her were client dinners he would spring on her at the last minute. Then again, there was that time he proposed to her. Then he did it again for the second time. The first time was just before the shooting. She never gave him an answer. She had no idea what she wanted to do. He was a wonderful man, but was he right for her? She didn't get butterflies in her stomach when he kissed her. She didn't smile at the sight of his name on her phone.

She had been in love before. That crazy kind of love. The kind that makes you feel like you could fly. The kind that makes you believe the entire world is yours for the taking. She wanted every moment of every day with him. The only problem with crazy love was what happened when it ended. Or in her case, it didn't end. It was years ago, yet the wound reopened whenever she pictured his stubbled face. She would love him until the day she died. She knew that with every stuttered beat of her damaged heart. Sadly, she also knew he would never change.

No matter how hard she loved him, she would never be enough. He wasn't the type of man to settle down. Fucking Peter Pan syndrome. Internally, she rolled her eyes. She wanted the opposite. She wanted to settle down. That's what she wanted more than anything. She was ready for a family.

After she returned from her month stay at Paxton's house, she came back even more determined to settle down. She knew Bentley would be a stable and committed husband, so what if things were only lukewarm with him?

That could change. Not everyone got the fairytale love story.

She'd said yes, ignoring the feeling in her gut. She hadn't yet told Paxton, and she knew he would be less than thrilled. He wasn't a fan of her new fiancé, even though they had never met in person. Another red flag. She'd never properly introduced him to her ragtag family.

He glanced over his shoulder at her before pouring his coffee. "You look exhausted, Krys. How long have you been up this time?"

"A few hours." She shrugged.

"You need to see a doctor. You can't keep going on like this. It's disruptive." He leaned against the kitchen counter. He sipped at the hot liquid in his mug.

"I've already been to see a doctor, remember?"

Setting the mug down, he crossed his arms over his chest. "Perhaps you should see a different one then. Someone who will prescribe you something to sleep at least."

She rolled her eyes. She hated when he talked to her like she needed to be told what to do. She was a grown ass woman, and if she wanted a man to boss her around, she would ask her brother his opinion on her life choices. He would happily oblige her.

"He said everything I'm experiencing is normal. I don't want to have to take something every night to sleep." She stood up, rounding the table to stand before him. "I took a man's life, Bentley."

"I told you to stop saying that. You make it sound like you murdered someone in cold blood. It was in defense of your friend Tori."

"Cori. Damn it, Bentley, my friend's name is Cori. How many times have I said that? Whether the circumstances were right or wrong, it doesn't change the outcome. My subconscious is trying to deal with it through my fucking dreams."

"This is getting nowhere. You obviously aren't going to listen to my advice on this and you know how I feel when you swear, Krys. We have more pressing matters to go over. I would like to formally announce our engagement at my father's dinner party after Thanksgiving." He pushed away from the counter, taking her arms in each hand. "We can discuss it more in detail later, I need to get going before I'm late for my meeting." He kissed her cheek, exiting the room before she could respond.

She stood there wondering, yet again, if she'd made the right decision in saying she would marry him. Then she remembered the pain she felt all those years ago. The pain of losing a love like no other, and it fortified her choice. He wouldn't hurt her that way. Her heart would be safe, at least. She needed to tell Paxton before it was on the front page of the society section of the paper. Not something she was looking forward to, but it was necessary.

Krysta figured no time like the present. She hustled to the bedroom. She needed a shower, and then she'd head to Bush Castle to have lunch with her big brother. She showered quickly, then grabbed a pair of jeans and a t-shirt from the drawer containing her things. She'd moved in a few weeks ago but decided to keep it quiet for now. Bentley worried it would look scandalous before the engagement was announced. People lived together before marrying all the time, she didn't see the big deal. He was afraid it would make the family look bad. Wait until his family got a good look at her tattooed covered, ex-cop, now private investigator brother and the rest of the gang she considered family. She giggled to herself. That was going to be fun.

Krysta turned down Paxton's street ninety minutes after leaving the house. His truck wasn't in the driveway, so she kept on going. He must be at the office. The ten-mile drive to Fear Incorporated went by in a haze of classic rock booming through her speakers.

Her brother retired from the police force a few years ago. Krysta didn't know everything about what happened to make him leave, but she knew enough to know his mental wellbeing couldn't take it anymore. One of his best friends started a private investigating firm and he was the first to jump aboard. Between the new job at Fear Incorporated and his life with Cori, Krysta couldn't remember a time her brother was as happy as he was now. She parked next to Paxton's truck and groaned as she walked past Kasper's motorcycle.

"Great," she mumbled.

She loved the guys. She really did. Kasper, however, knew every single button to push to make her lose her shit. All her shit. She was not in the mood to deal with him today. There was too much history there.

The bell above the door jingled as she entered the building. An adorable Mia waddled out from the back room. She wore a pink frilly dress that bounced around her as she ran toward Krysta. Krysta scooped the little angel up in her arms and spun her around.

She kissed Mia's forehead, breathing in the scent of baby shampoo. "Hey there, pretty girl." She loved being around the kids. They brought so much life and innocence into a gloomy world. Sometimes she wondered what kind of mother she would've been. She shook that thought away as quickly as it came. She didn't need to go down this road. Someday she'd have kids of her own. Her time hadn't run out yet. Not even close. She had plenty of it.

Putting Mia back down, she looked around the room. "Where's your mama?" The little girl cooed in response as she ran into the back. Sloane was nowhere in sight, but she was here looking for her brother anyway. He was sitting at his desk, talking animatedly. Where there's one, the other isn't usually far. So of course, Kasper was sitting right next to him.

His blue eyes bored into her from across the room. Like storm clouds rolling in, they were both beautiful and dangerous. Today, his chin-length locks were piled on his head in a messy man bun. She never understood his need to wear it that way. If it were up to her, she'd rip it out and suspend his hair tie privileges. She mentally rolled her eyes. Anything having to do with this man was definitely not her concern. Dread and butterflies fought for control of her belly as she squared her shoulders before marching toward them.

TWO
KASPER

KASPER GUTTENMUTH STARRED across the desk at his best friend Paxton, better known as Tank to his friends, in disbelief. "I'm sorry, what the fuck did you just say?"

Paxton crossed his muscular arms over his massive chest. "You heard me." Paxton gave him a defiant glare.

Kasper cocked an eyebrow. "Since when do you want to have holiday dinners and be all domesticated?"

"Since I found a good woman to settle down with. You do realize I'm done whoring around, right?"

"Yeah," he barked.

Deep down he knew. He just hadn't fully admitted it to himself yet. Who was he supposed to go out with on Friday nights now? He didn't want to go without a wing man. That was just sad. Bordering on pathetic. Really, he wasn't sure he wanted to go out at all anymore, but he was unattached, unlike half of his friends. Foster was married, Max might as well be, and now Tank was out of the game. That left Mother or Benji, and Benji was still undercover deep into Petrov's inner circle. Though last time he reported in, things were going well, but who knew when he would be around again?

"So, are you coming for dinner or what? I need a head count."

"Of course I am. If Doc is the one who's actually cooking the bird. You can grill like a champ, but I've never seen you use the oven except to warm left over pizza." Kasper chuckled.

"Fuck you, dude," Tank growled before grinning. "You really think Cori would let me cook?"

"I always knew she was a smart lady. Too smart for your dumbass."

"Don't tell her that, I don't want to risk her taking off again." They both laughed.

The Doc was a psychiatrist with a private practice before she moved to Bush Castle. She moved here to start over, only once she was here, she was held hostage in her own home by a guy whose wife she treated and subsequently lost to suicide. Tank's baby sister, Krysta, was the one who saved her. Before the man could carry out his plans to rape and kill Cori, Krysta put a bullet in the back of the bastard's head. He couldn't help the pride he'd felt in Krysta for sacrificing a piece of her soul to save another. Not that he had any right to feel prideful.

Once Doc was released from the hospital, she left town to stay with her sister. Leaving the big lug now sitting before him alone and miserable. That is until he found his balls and went after her. Now they spent every moment they could together, and Tank had been unsuccessfully trying to hide his newfound fascination with engagement rings.

Kasper would never admit he was slightly jealous. Tank was a new man. He was happy for the first time in a long time. Kasper could remember feeling that way. It seemed like another lifetime ago. Hell, it was. Back when he was barely more than a kid. It was an intoxicating feeling, but he'd fucked it all up. He was scared and handled everything the wrong way. Now she was gone. He had yet to feel one tenth of what he felt for her for any other woman. He tried on enough women to make the assumption he never would. She was one of a kind.

Too bad he still had to see her. More often than he wanted to. No, that wasn't right. He wanted to see her all the time, he just knew it would torture him every time he had to see her happy. One of these days she'd bring a guy home to meet Paxton. The thought made him want to puke. He wanted to be that guy.

"We were thinking an early dinner about three." Tank interrupted his thoughts. "Will that work for you?"

He scoffed. "Dude, you know there's no place else I'd rather be. I'll be there by noon to watch football with you all day."

Thanksgiving was only a week away. It was one of his favorite holidays. All the guys usually got together at Foster's house and Bella cooked for them. This year she was close to delivering their second child, and he figured Doc probably volunteered. It would be a nice change. The chime above the front door rang softly. He looked up. *Speak of the devil and she shall appear*, he thought.

Krysta stopped walking just long enough to hug Mia before making her way to where he was sitting. She looked fantastic. Her long chestnut hair was pulled back in a ponytail. She had legs for days. Once upon a time he knew firsthand just how soft they were. She was slender and toned, but not muscled. She loved running, usually on a treadmill. He could never understand that. He'd rather run outside where the scenery changed.

"Hey, big brother." She smiled at Tank. Tank got up from his chair and hugged her, lifting her clear off the ground.

"What a surprise." Tank's brow furrowed. "I didn't forget about a lunch date, did I?"

She giggled. "No. Though I won't lie and say that's not why I stopped in."

"Good, I'm glad I didn't fuck my schedule up again. This online calendar Cori set me up with," he shook his phone in his massive hand, "is great, but sometimes I forget to check the damn thing."

She giggled. The sound went straight to his balls. Somehow, her laugh was angelic and dirty at the same time. He flashed back to a time when she would lay in his arms naked as he regaled her with stories of the guys in the academy.

Kasper stood up from his perch on the edge of the desk. "What? No hello for me, Kitten?"

"Hello, ass face."

He grinned. "That's better."

Tank rolled his eyes at their exchange. "So anyway, I was actually going to call you today."

Krysta cocked her head in amusement. "You were?"

"Yeah, Cori and I have decided to host Thanksgiving dinner this year."

"Awesome. I was wondering how poor Bella was going to take on that task with a toddler and being so far along in this pregnancy. That's cool of you guys."

"You are coming this year, right?"

Kasper watched some of the color drain from her face. "Well...I'm not sure yet."

Tank took a step toward her. "You're kidding."

She smiled playfully. "Of course, I'll be there, but I might have to leave early."

"Fine."

Tank didn't sound incredibly pleased with her answer. Was Kasper missing out on something? Krysta never missed a holiday with Tank. Why would this one be any different.

Suddenly her face lit up. "Hey, maybe I should come down a day early. I can help Cori with lists of what will be needed, and I can help her shop and cook."

Tank beamed as he hugged her again. "I think Cori would really like that. I'd be pretty okay with it too." He winked.

"Great. That's settled then."

Kasper watched their exchange with interest just as he always did. He had a brother, but their relationship was never close. In fact, Kasper didn't even know where Kyle lived. He hadn't seen nor heard from him since Kasper had moved out at eighteen. They didn't have what you would call a happy childhood. Their father was a drunk and Kasper's mother had passed away when he was five. Just months before Jonas Guttenmuth remarried and had Kyle.

Kasper heard the old man died in a house fire a few years back. He passed out drunk while smoking and torched the place. He wished he could feel something about the passing of his father, but truth be told, he hated him. He wasn't sad the abusive bastard was gone. He spent most of his youth and teen years at Tank's house. He was always included in holidays and vacations. Mr. and Mrs. S were great people. He missed them as much as

Tank and Krysta. They were the only people who accepted him and treated him as one of their own.

Kasper smiled at Krysta. "Don't forget the pie, Kitten. You know how much I love pie."

A look of utter disgust painted her face. "You really are a pig."

Kasper's only reply was an oink sound. Tank barked with laughter, and he joined in. He loved fucking with her. That banter was established long before he knew what she tasted like. He saw no reason to not continue like nothing ever happened between them.

"Hey there, beautiful." Mortimer 'Mother' Neville wrapped his arms around Krysta. Kasper stopped laughing.

She kissed his cheek. "Hey Morty. It's always good to see you."

"Aren't you a sight. How have been holding up?"

"I'm doing okay." She smiled sadly.

"Well, don't forget, we're all family. If you need someone to talk to, I'm here."

She tucked a strand of hair behind her ear. "Thanks. You're a sweetheart. How is it that no woman has snapped you up yet?"

"They try." He winked. "I'm still waiting for you to come around."

"Flirt." She playfully pushed his shoulder.

"Stop hitting on my little sister," Tank growled with no seriousness behind it.

Mother kissed her cheek before heading back to his desk where he belonged. Tank's baby sister was all piss and vinegar on the outside. Shit, she was mostly piss and vinegar on the inside too. Her soft side was buried under the emotional debris of years and years of torment from

Tank and himself. He wondered if anyone knew it was there at all.

Tank sat back down in his chair. "Hey, you never did say why you came by. It's not like you were in the neighborhood."

Yeah, he hadn't thought about that. Kasper was so used to Krysta being around he sometimes forgot how far away she lived. She seemed nervous for some reason. Standing up, he was ready to go to her, but she smiled brightly. It was such a change that Kasper thought he must've imagined the nervousness.

"It's nothing really. I thought maybe you'd want to grab some lunch."

He frowned. "I'd love to, but I have to be in court in an hour."

"Don't worry about it. Another time. I'm going to head out. Maybe I'll swing by and see Cori before I head back. I think I have some of Mom's old recipes at home. I'll see if I can't dig them up this week."

Tank rubbed his hands together. "That's awesome. Drive safe."

"Will do." Krysta turned to go. Kasper scurried over to her, taking hold of her arm. She stopped walking and looked down at his hand holding her, a blank mask in place hinting at nothing.

"Yes?"

He leaned in so close his lips almost brushed her ear. She smelled fucking amazing. Like vanilla with a hint of earthiness. "Don't forget the pie, Kitten."

Krysta's cheeks blushed slightly. Direct hit. He mentally cheered himself on. She squared her shoulders, staring him in the eye. The mask gone, fire blazed in her eyes. "You don't need any pie from me, Kass. I'm sure the ladies are lined up to give you theirs."

She pulled out of his grasp and marched out of the building. He stood there for a moment watching the empty doorway. He'd have that sweet scent stuck in his mind all day. He took a deep breath and pasted a smile on his face, as he made his way back to Tank's desk.

Tank looked up. "What was that all about?"

"Just messin' with her."

"Don't you ever get tired of pissing her off?"

Kasper pretended to ponder his question, his fingertips scratching at the stubble on his chin. "Now that you mention it...nope." He grinned.

"One of these days, man, she's gonna chew you up and spit you out."

Kasper walked back to his own desk to get some work done, mumbling on the way there. "Too late."

———

Two hours later he was sitting on a park bench in downtown Bush Castle, watching a grown man play volleyball like he was on the girls' junior varsity team. It was disgraceful to men everywhere. Hell, it was disgraceful to women everywhere. Nonchalantly, Kasper used the camera on his cell phone to take a video of the man attempting to spike the ball across the net.

Frederick Jones looked awfully active for a man who couldn't work due to a fall at the warehouse he was employed at. Even though it was out of the scope of Kasper's job description, he snapped a few shots of Mr. Jones with his face buried in some cleavage that certainly didn't belong to Mrs. Jones. His range of motion looked simply fine to him.

Kasper uploaded the images to a folder and emailed them to his work email. That was easier than he thought. He figured he'd have to follow the guy around for a few days at least. It was nice of the guy to make it easy on him. He didn't feel like going back to the office just yet. He only had a report to write, and since he was a few days ahead of schedule, he decided to take the rest of the day off. It was time for him to grab some grub.

There was a little bar and grill two blocks over that had amazing burgers. That sounded damn good right about now. The place was always crowded at lunchtime. He took the last seat available at the bar.

"Hey, sugar," Shari cooed from across the mahogany counter as she handed him a menu.

"I didn't know you worked here. I'll take a Sprite to start." Shari was looking at him like he was dessert. She was a lot of fun for a weekend years ago, but he wasn't interested in a repeat.

"Now you know, so don't be a stranger."

Once his bacon lover's burger was ordered, he took a sip of his Sprite and surveyed the room. A familiar laugh drew his attention and he quickly found its owner. He couldn't believe his eyes. John Danbry was sitting across the table from Krysta, smiling like he had the coveted answer to the meaning of life. Kasper's blood began to boil. John was a grade A prick in high school. Kasper couldn't count how many times Krysta had come home from a date with John in tears. Paxton had once told him it was because John was pressuring her to have sex and when she wouldn't, he would break it off long enough to get laid then crawl back to her. It took Kasper threatening to ram his teeth down his throat for John to stop calling her.

Kasper called to the bartender, "I'll be right back." She nodded.

Kasper strolled over to their table with a big smile on his face. They'd obviously been here for a while. Empty plates littered the table. He shoved his hands in his pockets to keep himself in check. "Johnny, hey buddy. Long time no see." John's fingers twitched, giving away his uneasiness.

"Hey, man. It has been a while."

Krysta continued to stare daggers at him. "Hey, Kitten. I thought you were stopping by Tank's and heading home. That was a couple hours ago."

Her smile was laced with contempt. "I was, but then I ran into John while getting gas and he asked me to lunch."

John sat silently listening to their exchange, along with every table within ear shot. His eyes volleyed between them.

Now Kasper was getting pissed for no reason other than seeing her with another guy. One who had treated her like shit almost a decade ago, no less. "Need I remind you how many times this asshole made you cry?"

"That was almost ten years ago, Kasper. We aren't kids anymore, and to be honest, it's none of your fucking business."

"None of my…that's where you're wrong."

Krysta stood abruptly. Her chair squealed loudly as her legs pushed it away. People were trying not to stare. They weren't succeeding. "John, thank you for a lovely lunch. It was nice catching up, but I really must be going."

John stood as well. Stuffing his hands in his front pockets. "It was great seeing you."

Kasper called after her. "See you at Thanksgiving dinner, Kitten."

She flipped him off as she stormed out of the restaurant. A few customers laughed at their exchange before whispering to their companions.

Kasper turned back to John. "Stay the fuck away from her. I don't care if it's been ten years or fifty."

Without waiting for a reply, Kasper hurried to the bar. Shari was waiting with a perfectly arched eyebrow. He threw a twenty-dollar bill on the counter. "I'll be back."

Krysta was opening her car door by the time he caught up to her in the parking lot behind the pub. She stopped, her car door hanging open. Putting her hands on her hips, she glared at him. She was pissed, which only made her more attractive. Didn't that make him all the more of a dick for thinking so?

"What *is* your problem?" she spat.

"My problem? You were the one enjoying a meal with a guy who constantly pressured you for sex and broke your heart because you wouldn't. So, what was that about?"

She huffed, "That was forever ago. He was a horny teenage boy, and I was a scared virgin—which I certainly am not anymore."

No, she was not. He saw to that personally. She'd been nervous as hell that first time, but so fucking responsive. Her body given freely for him to do with as he pleased. She was perfect. His pants started to tighten with the memory.

He knew what he was about to do was a bad fucking idea, but he couldn't stop himself. She'd been around a lot lately and it was getting harder to control himself. He kept moving forward even as his brain yelled *stop*. Without a word, he took Krysta's face in his hands. He closed the last bit of distance between them and pressed his lips against hers.

Her sweet smell enveloped him. The skin beneath his fingertips was as smooth as silk, but it was her lips that captivated him. Her lips were still as soft as ever. It was just like the first time he kissed her seven years ago. He felt their kiss to the tips of his toes. No one before or since could make him come unglued the way she did. He slid his hands into her hair, gripping firmly as he angled her head where he wanted it. Her hands fisted his shirt. Growling, he pushed his tongue into her mouth. Her taste was truly intoxicating. He hadn't yet stopped kissing her and already he was looking forward to the next time.

Suddenly, Krysta pushed him away, her breath coming in rapid pants. It was good to know he still had that effect on her. He couldn't describe the look in her eyes, though. Surprise, anger, desire. A mix of all three fluttered across her face before landing on anger.

"This is one notch you already have on your belt."

She lowered herself into her car and shut the door. She never even glanced his direction as she drove out of the parking lot. He stood there watching after her even after she was long gone. She was never a notch on his belt. He fucked things up royally back then. He knew that. Maybe he could convince her to give him another chance? A real chance this time. No hiding, no secrets.

It wouldn't be easy, but they say nothing worth having ever is. She was worth everything. Smiling to himself, with his mind made up, he went back inside the pub to eat.

THREE
KRYSTA

HE HAD a lot of fucking nerve. To think he could interrupt her lunch *and* kiss her. What the hell was wrong with him? He'd made his mind up about them years ago. It took a long time for her to get over him. No way was she playing these games again.

She was marrying Bentley. She pulled over in the first parking lot she came to. Laying her head back onto the head rest, she closed her eyes, and it all came flooding back again.

He smiled at her from across the room. It wasn't the fake smile he wore for all the girls he flirted with. It was real and it was beautiful. Paxton put his arm around his best friend and the moment was gone.

Kasper winked at her playfully. "Who are you all dolled up for, Kitten?"

She wasn't dolled up per se. Who was she kidding? She was all dressed up because she was going on a date. She secretly wished it were Kasper taking her out, but she knew that would never happen. That didn't mean she wouldn't show him what he was missing even if he barely registered she was female. She was just Paxton's little sister to him.

"I'm going to the movies."

A horn honked outside. Paxton looked out the window. "That doesn't look like Marcia's car."

She rolled her eyes at her nosey brother. "That's because it's not Marcia. It's John."

Both boys whipped their head in her direction so fast they looked like cartoon characters. She practically doubled over with laughter. "The look on your faces," she cackled.

"Seriously?" Her poor sweet brother actually looked confused for a moment.

"John Danby?" Kasper scoffed before continuing without her confirmation. "He's a prick. You aren't dating him," he ordered.

Krysta stopped laughing. He was serious. "Excuse me?"

"Kasper's right. He's been with half the girls in school. No way."

"So what? So, have you two."

"That's not the point."

"Both of you can kiss my ass. I can go out with anyone I choose. Now if you'll excuse me, I have a date waiting." She glared at them. "I'm leaving, Mom! I'll be home by curfew."

"Have fun," her mom yelled from the kitchen.

She stormed out of the house. John waved from inside the car, a big smile spread across his face. She slipped in the passenger side, risking a glance back at her house. Kasper was staring at her from the living room window, arms crossed over his chest with a scowl on his face. It was eerie and chilled her to the bone. She wrapped her arms around herself as they drove away.

Krysta wiped a tear from her cheek, putting the car in drive. Just like back then, Kasper thought he could boss her around. That wasn't happening. She needed to stop letting him get to her. It didn't matter how much she liked the feel of his lips on hers or how her heart raced around him. Her heart barely survived the first time. She had no doubt he would destroy her given another chance.

She parked her car in Paxton's driveway behind Cori's. She opened the screen door to find the inside door cracked open. That was odd. Cori usually had the house locked up like Fort Knox after her ordeal. She never left doors open when Paxton was gone.

Cori had been stalked and attacked by a former patient's husband. Krysta was grateful for getting to her and her brother in time to save them, even if taking a man's life had plagued her with nightmares ever since.

Unease bubbled in Krysta's gut. "Cori?" she whispered. Reaching behind her, she slipped her Ruger from the holster at the small of her back.

Cori cautiously entered the living room. She looked around slowly. "Are you okay?"

"Yeah, why?"

"You have your gun drawn." Cori eyed the piece in Krysta's hand. "Why the hell are we whispering?"

Realization hit Krysta. She laughed loudly, concealing her pistol once again. She wore it everywhere since the day of the attack. It was an everyday staple. Keys, check. Phone, check. Ruger, check. "I have no idea. I was worried, the door was unlocked."

"Oh! Tank texted me and said you were in town and might stop by. You're later than I expected, though."

"I ran into an old friend at the gas station, and we had lunch."

Cori wagged her eyebrows. "A male friend?'

"It's not what you're thinking." She laughed. "How are you holding up?"

"Some days are better than others. When Tank is on a stake out late it can be hard, but I'm doing okay. How about you? Are the nightmares any better?"

Krysta shrugged. "They're still pretty consistent."

Cori closed the space between them, wrapping her in a hug. She smelled like lavender and Krysta felt some of the tension leave her shoulders.

"It takes time and work. You don't heal overnight. Even I have to remind myself sometimes."

"I'm trying to be patient with myself. It's just frustrating some days. I always wonder if I could have done anything differently, even though I know I did the only thing I could to keep you both safe."

"That's completely normal, Krysta."

"So, on a happier note, I'm gonna come stay with you guys a few days to help you."

"I would love that. I've never had to cook a big meal for so many people. I could definitely use all the help I can get." She giggled.

"I have some old recipes from my mom. I'll dig them out and bring them with me."

"How's the boyfriend feel about you spending time here?"

"Actually, I haven't told him yet. I'm sure he'll be fine with it." She shrugged her shoulders. Bentley was secure enough in their relationship to not worry about what she did. Unless he needed an escort for a fundraiser or some such event, he didn't mind when she did her own thing. "At least he won't have to wear earplugs to bed for a few days."

Cori scrunched her nose. "Earplugs?"

"Sometimes I cry or yell in my sleep. It disturbs his rest, so now he wears earplugs so he can sleep through my nightmares."

Cori looked at her like she was crazy. "And you don't see anything wrong with that?"

"He needs his rest."

"You need someone to be there for you. Someone who supports your recovery."

"It's fine."

"If that's the bullshit you want to feed yourself, go ahead."

"He's a good man." Krysta could feel herself beginning to boil on the inside.

"I never he said he wasn't. Having said that, being a good man doesn't mean he's good for you."

Krysta had no good argument to deny what Cori said. A part of her knew Cori was right, while the other cared deeply for Bentley. Well, as much as she could care about anyone. So, she tried lightening the conversation up. "Well, not everyone can have a perfect man like Paxton."

"That man is far from perfect."

As if he were conjured, Paxton walked through the door. "Who's not perfect?"

The girls laughed together. "You, big brother. News flash, you aren't perfect."

"Well, I'd say that's the opinion of a bratty ass little sister. Therefore, invalid." He winked. "So, what have you been up to since you left the office?"

"Actually, I bumped into Danbry and had lunch." Krysta braced herself for his overreaction.

"How's John doing? I haven't seen him in a few months."

"Wait, you aren't going to get all Cro-Magnon brother on me?" Like your idiot best friend, Kasper, she thought.

"Why would I? John's an okay guy and you're an adult now." He shrugged. "You could do worse. Speaking of, how are things with your guy?"

Really? Doing worse made him think of Bentley? She mentally rolled her eyes.

"Bentley and I are just fine."

"Just fine, huh?"

He gave her the perfect opening to tell him about her engagement. She panicked though. "I'd rather not talk about it."

"Fair enough, for now." Her brother threw an arm around her shoulder. "How's work? We barely had time to speak when you stopped by."

"Great, I'm ahead of schedule on all of my projects."

"Impressive."

Cori put her hands on her hips. "Sleep deprivation will do that for you."

She shot Cori a pointed look. Snitch.

Paxton glared at her. Worry etched into his strong face. "Still not sleeping right?"

"Some nights are difficult," she lied. It was more like most nights. She didn't want him to worry any more than he already did.

They sat and talked over coffee for a while until Krysta noticed the time. "I better run, guys. I'll be back in a few days." She hugged them both before heading home.

She loved being here with them. If it weren't for Bentley, she would seriously consider relocating. Bush Castle was a good place to grow up in. If she ever had kids, this was the type of town she would want to raise them in.

There was crime everywhere, but in Bush Castle, major crimes were low. Mostly petty crimes and misdemeanors.

The drive home went by quickly. Pulling into her driveway, she felt exhaustion wash over her. Cori was right. She needed to remember to give herself time. Not only to recover from the incident, but from the guilt she felt. Yawning, she unlocked the front door and entered. She walked through the living room into the spacious kitchen. She set her keys on the counter, then retrieving a glass from the cupboard, she poured a glass of wine. Bentley wasn't home yet. That wasn't unusual.

She had lived in a small, one-bedroom apartment before moving in with Bentley. This place was a modest sized two-bedroom rancher that cost too damn much for its size. However, the view made up for it. Pushing the curtain aside and unlocking the sliding door, Krysta stepped out onto the small, wooden deck. The unseasonably warm breeze whipped her ponytail around. She sipped her sangria, taking a moment to soak in the view. The city twinkled on the horizon in a sea of colored lights. There wasn't much of a yard, and what was there sloped down, forming a hill. Sitting in one of the two wicker chairs, she took a deep breath. This was the only place in the house where she felt at peace.

Once her glass was empty, she went back inside. Maybe tonight she could get some sleep.

FOUR
KASPER

SWINGING A LEG UP AND OVER, Kasper sat on the leather seat of his black Harley Davidson Fatboy. Adjusting his helmet, he kicked up the stand, and took off out of town. Sometimes he would ride around for hours. Being on his bike calmed him when nothing else could. He needed to find a little calm today.

Seeing Krysta a few days ago still had him knotted up inside. It's not like they hadn't seen each other a million times in the past. She was his best friend's little sister. They were staples in each other's lives. Even after he fucked things up years ago, they remained in orbit of each other. He couldn't pinpoint why this visit had affected him to this degree. Why did he kiss her? He was a glutton for fucking punishment, that's why.

He steered the twists and turns almost without thought, muscle memory leading him on a familiar journey. Spotting the open shoulder he was searching for, he pulled his steel horse over, turning the key and removing it from the ignition. The small foot path was undiscernible unless you were looking for it. Kasper knew exactly where he was going.

Ducking overgrown branches and stepping over fallen ones, he trudged through the woods. Most of the trees sported leaves of red, yellow, and orange, if any at all. The forest floor reminded him of a mosaic vase Mrs. S had in their dining room when he was growing up. Stepping out from the trees, he entered a clearing.

The clearing stretched out about five hundred feet before dropping off the cliff's edge. Kasper took a deep breath. The breeze blew his long hair around his head. Pulling it back into an elastic band, he walked closer to the edge before sitting down on the grass. This was his sanctuary. If anyone else knew about this place, he was none the wiser. He'd never seen a soul. The view below was spectacular, but it had never been more beautiful than the only woman he'd ever brought here.

Krysta's eyes sparkled as he removed the blindfold. The sun was setting on their small town, painting the deep blue sky with ribbons of red and purple. Standing there near the cliff's edge, eyes wide with wonderment, Krysta beamed up at him. She was so damn beautiful; Kasper could barely catch his breath.

"It's gorgeous," she whispered. "How did you find this place?"

"By accident. A couple years back."

Kasper slung the backpack off his back, then unzipped it and removed a folded blanket. Spreading it out, he sat down, patting the spot next to him. Krysta plopped down with a giggle. She put her head on his shoulder as they watched the sun fade away.

The stars were clear and bright this far away from anything. Kasper felt as if they were the only two people left on Earth. He had stolen a few kisses from her over the last couple of months. He wanted her to kiss him. He wanted just a taste of what it was like to be wanted by this woman.

As if hearing his thoughts, she lifted her head, and stretching up to him, she placed her sweet lips to his. She climbed onto his lap without ending the kiss. It only intensified. Their tongues danced in perfect unison.

His cock stiffened under her. She began to rock against him. He threaded one hand into her silky hair, the other gripped her hip, urging her to continue. He wanted to be inside of her more than anything. That scared him, but not enough to say no when she reached down to unbutton his jeans.

She sat back on his thighs as she unzipped him. Her eyes fixated on her task, she slowly freed his cock. The warm breeze blew her hair around like a wild headdress as she bit her bottom lip. She looked like magic.

That first time would live in his mind forever. He was wrong, one taste wasn't enough. He didn't think it ever would be. Sighing, he shoved his hands in his pockets and continued to take in the beauty before him. This was their place. He wondered if they would ever see it together again.

Following the familiar trail, Kasper made it back to his bike in no time. The engine roared to life beneath him. He headed back to town, leaving this little trip down memory lane behind him.

———

Thanksgiving was in two days. Max decided to close the shop until Monday, giving everyone time to enjoy the holiday. He'd met Max almost a decade ago in the police academy. They were fresh out of high school when they thought they could change the world. Kasper had planned on wearing blue until his dying day. What he didn't plan on was the politics and backstabbing that went on.

After the McGregor case, Max and Tank left the precinct. Max's injury meant a desk job and he wasn't having that. Tank just said fuck it and quit. It didn't take long before Kasper felt as if his skin was too tight every time he walked into the building. He knew, like Tank, it was time for a change.

Life had a funny way of working out though. He loved working with Max and the guys. He knew without a doubt he could trust every man on this team with his life, and he would give his life for any of them.

"Hey numb nuts," Kasper called out as he walked through Tank's front door.

Cori squealed as she pushed Tank's head out from between her thighs. Straightening her skirt, she stormed out of the room, mumbling. Kasper was pretty certain she called him a dick. Tank shot him a death glare from where he was still on his knees, wiping his mouth with his hand.

"What the fuck, man?" He pushed himself up to his feet.

"Sorry." He laughed.

"I told you, you gotta knock now. This is the second time this month."

"At least I didn't get a view of your hairy ass this time."

"Cori is gonna kill you." He grinned, wiping his face with his palm.

"Nah, she loves me," Kasper yelled loud enough for Cori to hear him.

"Not right now she doesn't," she called out.

Tank smiled, walking into the kitchen. Kasper followed him, finding Cori riffling through the fridge.

"Looks like I'm just in time for lunch."

"You're like a truffle pig, you know that?" Cori asked.

"I've been called a pig a few times, but never a truffle pig."

"You can sniff out anytime we're about to have a meal." She laughed, shaking her head side to side. "There's roast beef and turkey."

She continued retrieving lunchmeat, cheese, and condiments from the fridge as Tank grabbed a package of round rolls fresh from the bakery.

"You got any of that good ass horseradish sauce?"

"Hell yeah," Tank replied.

"It's a good day." Kasper rubbed his hands together in anticipation.

Tank sliced open a roll. Turning to Cori, he grinned. "Hand me that meat, Momma."

"Isn't that her line?" Kasper deadpanned.

Handing over the packages of lunchmeat, Cori sighed. "You two are incorrigible."

"Maybe." Tank smirked.

"Probably," Kasper replied. "Are we deep frying the turkey this year?"

"I already told Paxton no."

"Aww…come on, Ma." Kasper whined like a little kid.

"Absolutely not. I'm roasting the turkey. I'm not spending Thanksgiving in the ER due to third degree burns."

Tank scoffed. "Ye of little faith."

Cori pinned him with a look. It might be scary to other men, but not them. At least he didn't think so. He was surprised, though. Tank stopped what he was doing, making eye contact with his very annoyed girlfriend. He turned his attention back to his sandwich art. "So, anyway, Cori is roasting the turkey."

Kasper whispered, "Pussy."

"Eat your sandwich and shut up," Tank growled.

Kasper took an outrageous bite, winking at the two of them.

"Did Krysta mention if she's bringing anyone for Thanksgiving?" Cori asked as she made her own sandwich.

"Why would she?" Kasper asked, afraid of what the answer would be.

"Because she's been seeing someone."

Kasper turned to Tank. "You know what she's talking about?"

"She mentioned a guy a while back."

A while back? How long? Was she involved when she was here last time? Fuck. He wouldn't have kissed her if he'd known. That might've been a lie. He couldn't have stopped himself.

"What's he like? Another douche we gotta run off? Just say when and where."

"Dunno. Never met him. It's not serious. At least, not that I know of."

"Seriously? You haven't insisted to meet him?" That surprised Kasper. Tank was like a momma hen with Krysta. How the hell was he supposed to get answers now?

"When she's ready, I'll meet him." Tank shrugged. "She's not a child anymore. She can make up her own mind when it comes to who she spends time with."

Cori gave him a look he couldn't decipher. "Neanderthal."

Kasper shook his head. That didn't sound like his best friend at all. Cori brought out a whole other side to him. He remembered a time when he wanted to be a better version of himself. Krysta had made him want to be better. To be a man who deserved her love. In the end, he proved he wasn't worthy of her at all. That got him thinking. What kind of guy would Krysta date now? Would the guy remind her of him? Or would he be the exact opposite? *Opposite*, he said to himself.

"Dude…" Tank snapped his fingers in front of Kasper's face. Sitting down on a stool, Tank took a bite of his sandwich.

"What?" How long had he zoned out for?

"I said, don't go giving her any shit when she gets here tomorrow."

"Now does that sound like something I'd do?" He smirked.

"You boys stay outta trouble. I'm going to get the spare room cleaned up for her." Cori kissed the top of Tank's shaved head before leaving the two of them on their own.

Kasper wanted to come clean with Paxton over the years. He just couldn't find the words. How do you tell your best friend you're in love with his baby sister without him wanting to pummel your ass? You don't. He was in love. Tank was going to kill him. *Shit.*

He already proved he wasn't worth her time. There was no way she'd change her mind and give him another chance. Especially not if she was seeing someone.

FIVE
KRYSTA

IT WAS THANKSGIVING MORNING. Krysta was excited to spend the day with Cori, Sloane, and little Mia, while Max and Kasper hung out with Paxton. Foster and Marabella would be there after Seth woke up from a nap this afternoon. She threw her long hair up into a bun before hurrying downstairs. Cori was in the kitchen staring at the unwrapped turkey with terror in her eyes.

"Is everything okay?"

"No. I have no idea what I'm doing." Cori threw her hands up in the air with an exaggerated sigh. "I haven't even had my coffee yet."

Krysta chuckled as she walks over. "Let me help. I'll get the bird ready; you make the coffee."

"I can handle that. Why did I think I could do this on my own?"

"You can, but you aren't. We'll do it together."

It took longer than Krysta thought it would to get the turkey prepped, but she was proud of herself. Cori looked over her shoulder.

"No stuffing in there? On television it's always stuffed."

"I stuffed it with onions, carrots, and apples. Our mom always made the stuffing separate. She said the turkey didn't dry out that way."

Paxton entered the kitchen. Kissing Cori, he studied the turkey. "Look at you. Mom would be proud."

They shared a look before she hugged her brother tightly. She felt tears pool in her eyes. She blinked rapidly, hoping Paxton wouldn't notice. They missed their parents all the time, but holidays were especially rough. This year, she was feeling a little closer to her mom. She could imagine her giving out orders and nagging Krysta about her boyfriend and how his absence was noted. She wished her mom were here to nag her. It should have told her something about her relationship that she didn't miss Bentley's presence.

"You think so?"

"I know so."

"Can you handle putting the bird in the oven for us?"

Kasper came through the kitchen door. "What's this about a bird?" he asked cheerfully.

Krysta flipped him the middle finger. "I was saying how I had one for you, now you ruined the surprise."

"Cute, Kitten."

Why did he have to be so damn hot? He was wearing a deep green button-down shirt. She wondered if he remembered it was her favorite color. *Doubtful.* She internally scoffed. She was a short chapter in the book of debauchery that was Kasper Guttenmuth's autobiography.

Paxton shook his head like usual at their banter. "You're here early. I thought you said noon."

"Yeah." Kasper shrugs. "I woke up earlier than I

thought, so I figured I'd come rile the Kitten up a bit." He waggled his eyebrows at Krysta.

"You're a man-child, Ass Face."

"Enough. It's Thanksgiving. Let's try to be civil."

Krysta stuck her tongue out at Kasper. Cori laughed before pouring Krysta a cup of coffee. She sniffed the mug, sighing. "Thanks, Cori." After adding some cream—okay, a lot of cream—she walked outside to sit on the porch. She could hear the three of them laughing inside.

She hated to leave tomorrow. This was the only time she felt like herself. It was also the first night she hadn't been woken up by a nightmare in months. She felt safe and loved. She could work from anywhere. The only thing holding her back was Bentley. He couldn't leave. Without asking, she knew he wouldn't want to, either. His father and their connections were important to his future in politics.

She closed her eyes, swaying on the porch swing. The birds chirped as she soaked in the peacefulness around her.

———

"Krysta, we're going to be eating leftovers for a month," Cori exclaimed. "What are you making now?"

"Sweet potato casserole."

"We already have potatoes cooking to mash."

"So?"

"So, who's gonna eat all of this?"

Laughing at her friend, she looked like the top of her head might explode. Krysta put her arm around Cori's shoulder. "Listen, we're going to have four grown men here. You've seen each of them eat, especially my brother.

When you add the women and kids, that's eleven people. We'll be lucky if there are leftovers."

"I didn't think about that," Cori responded, calmly this time.

"See, it's all good. The turkey is almost done. Why don't we set the table?"

"I couldn't have done this without you. Thank you."

Cori threw her arms around Krysta, squeezing tightly. She knew one day Cori was going to be her sister-in-law. Tank was dumb sometimes, but he wasn't stupid. She couldn't have been happier. They were perfect together. They had the kind of love people wrote stories about. She didn't want to acknowledge she may have had that and lost it years ago.

"It's my pleasure."

"Did someone say pleasure?" Kasper asked as he strolled into the kitchen. It was like he had a sixth sense. "Anything I can help you with, Kitten?"

"Don't you wish."

"You know it." He winked playfully. Her insides did not get gooey.

Rolling her eyes, she grabbed a stack of plates, and carried them to the dining table. Surprisingly, Kasper was right behind her, bringing the glasses in. She reached out, taking them from him, her fingers brushing his. Their eyes met. She'd been lost in those beautiful orbs before. She was helpless to stop herself. It was as if the past few years had never even happened. She was drowning. Deeper and deeper into the abyss. Thank God for the doorbell breaking Kasper's spell.

Tank scurried to the door. His excitement was contagious. Krysta smiled, thinking about how happy her brother finally was. The house boomed with laughter. The kids screamed in delight as "Uncle Pax" chased them around, growling like a beast. Kasper grinned as he joined Paxton. The squeals doubled as Marabella and Sloane joined her in the dining room.

"Can we help?" Sloane asked.

"I never turn down help to set the table."

It was good to be surrounded by family. Krysta couldn't remember the last time she felt so content. She loved the sound of the kids' laughter. Standing there, watching them longingly, she gave herself a rare moment to imagine what could have been.

"I'm sorry," he whispered only for her to hear.

She straightened her shoulders, mustering all her strength. "It wasn't meant to be."

"What if it was?"

Turning toward him, she studied his face. He had to be joking. What the hell was he up to now? He walked out on her when she needed him the most. That wasn't something she was ready to let go of. Was this some part of a midlife crisis? They weren't that old, but it was the only explanation she could come up with.

"Look, I don't know what you're talking about."

"I was wrong."

"Well, that's a given. You usually are."

She liked their witty banter better than this serious shit. She decided to walk away while she could. Kasper pulled her back. He cupped her face with both hands. Sparks ignited everywhere his hands touched. His gaze locked on hers, his stormy blue eyes hypnotizing her. The room fell away. She was deaf to everything but their breathing. It was her and Kasper. A smirk slowly lifted the left side of his full lips. The same one he'd given her in the past, usually right before he would steal a kiss. She should move, should break this spell he obviously had her under.

If he kissed her now, she would be helpless to control the emotions she kept buried inside. She wouldn't be able to push him away like she did in the parking lot the other day. That had used up the rest of her willpower. If he kissed her, she'd kiss him back. Her brother would lose his shit. She wouldn't recover from another Kasper-induced heartache. She'd barely survived the first time. She needed to step back. She couldn't, though. Her head said danger, but her heart begged her to stay. Her heart was obviously dumb. His thumbs brushed across her cheeks gently.

"Ahem."

The spell broken, Krysta turned toward the sound, forcing Kasper to drop his hands. Paxton raised an eyebrow. *Fucking great.* She didn't have time to deal with him, not when Bentley was glaring at her from the doorway. Bentley, fuck. He never even surfaced in her mind. She was a horrible person. How could she have completely forgotten?

"Bentley, what are you doing here?"

Scurrying over to him, Krysta kissed his cheek. He continued to scowl at Kasper before whispering in her ear, "I thought I'd surprise you and we could head back together after dinner."

She had already told him she wouldn't be home until tomorrow. She wasn't a fan of him showing up to try to make her leave—even if he did save her from making a horrible mistake.

"Gonna introduce us to your friend, Kitten?" Kasper's voice had more of a growl to it.

Krysta straightened her shoulders, glaring at Kasper. He was a smug bastard, standing there smiling. His fake smile at that. She wanted to punch him. She slipped her arm through Bentley's.

"Everyone, this is Bentley, my boyfriend." He gave her a raised eyebrow. *Shit, fiancé.*

Paxton shook Bentley's hand. "It's good to finally meet you face to face. I'm Krysta's brother, Paxton. Everyone just calls me Tank."

"Nice meeting you."

She watched Bentley's face as he took in the beastly man that was her brother. She almost missed the cringe as he took in the sleeves of tattoos and Paxton's shaved head. Almost.

Krysta introduced Bentley around the room to everyone individually. Everyone except Kasper, and Cori seemed genuinely surprised. Of course, they would, she didn't parade her love life around, like someone else she knew. Another reminder of how Kasper would only hurt her in the end. He didn't do monogamy.

She tried to smile sweetly.

"I need to check on dinner. Do you want a drink?"

"Nah, I'm good for now." Bentley eyed her suspiciously.

She scurried out of the living room, hoping for a moment of peace, however, she could feel someone right on her heels. She knew who that could be just by the gooseflesh on her body.

"Boyfriend, huh?"

"So? I *can* have a boyfriend, Kasper. I'm not a little girl."

"Tank mentioned it," he growled. "I know damn well you're not a little girl."

"Good."

"Is it serious?" he asked as he walked slowly toward

her. So fucking slow and casual. Like he wasn't causing her stomach to do somersaults. He unbuttoned his left shirt sleeve, rolling it up to his elbow. *No. Just no.* Some women liked butts. Some liked eyes. Krysta went crazy for a well sculpted set of forearms. In conjunction with rolled sleeves, it was like fucking kryptonite. This asshole knew it.

She felt as though a predator was stalking her. Maybe he was a predator in his own way where she was considered. His eyes bored into her, waiting for an answer, his right sleeve now rolled to match the other. Her treacherous heart sped up the closer he got. She had to fight not to look at his now bare forearms.

"It's not really any of your business."

He came around the island counter and up behind her. Placing both hands on the countertop, he blocked her in. She snuck a peek at the arms trapping her. *Fuck. Absolute perfection.* Kasper leaned in, brushing his nose along her ear as he whispered, "Is it serious?" He enunciated each word with a clenched jaw, his fingers turning white with the pressure he was putting on them.

Her eyes fluttered closed. She couldn't look at them anymore. Gooseflesh pebbled her skin as she held her breath, waiting to see what he would do next. She should push him away. She knew she should. Put some much-needed distance between them, but she was frozen. It was always this way with them. This untamed electricity jumping back and forth between their bodies.

"Am I interrupting?" Bentley asked from the doorway.

Her eyes popped open, and she released the breath she'd been holding. Kasper didn't move from behind her. If anything, he leaned in closer.

Shaking her head, she finally managed to make her

feet move. She squeezed past Kasper to stand away from both of them. Going to the fridge to busy herself, she grabbed a bottle of water. She needed to cool down anyway. Not that she would admit that. "No, of course not."

"You looked rather enthralled," Bentley accused, crossing his arms across his chest.

Kasper grinned. "Were you enthralled, Kitten?"

She shot him what she hoped was a death glare. "I was not. I was contemplating how much jail time I'd get if I stabbed you."

"I hate to break it to you, but Bradley doesn't look like he believes you."

"It's Bentley. Can I have a few moments with my fiancé? In private."

"Kitten?"

"Of course, you can go now, Kass."

Bentley stood in front of her, his hands on his hips now. It was his only tell when he was angry. He was a politician's son. He had learned early to keep his emotions in check. He didn't say anything for what seemed like hours, but she knew it was only a minute. The silence was deafening. "Is there something going on with that guy I should know about?"

"No, there isn't."

"It doesn't seem that way. He was practically all over you. Why the hell does he keep calling you kitten?"

"He wasn't even touching me. We've been friends since we were kids, for fuck's sake. He's like a second annoying brother. The nickname has been a way to get under my skin since I was a bratty teen."

No one knew about their relationship. Not a soul. She had to tell Bentley someday, but not today, not where everyone could overhear and know her secret. Once they were back home, she would tell him everything.

"He doesn't look at you like a little sister," he yelled, his mask cracking. She'd never seen him act this way. Bentley was always in control. It was one of the things that drove her crazy. They never fought. He said what was on his mind, and for him, it was law. She wasn't one who had the law laid out for her, yet again making her question why she'd accepted his proposal in the first place.

"Can we please have this conversation later, where people aren't eavesdropping?"

"Don't think for one second that every person out there doesn't see it, Krysta. Is this why you haven't told them about my proposal? Are you waiting for him? I can't afford a scandal. You need to talk to me."

Ahhh, that's what this is about. A potential scandal. She took a deep breath. Before she could respond, Tank appeared in the kitchen. His arms were crossed over his chest. Not a good sign.

"Is there a problem in here?" His voice was dangerously low and calm. Her brother was like a coiled snake ready to strike without a moment's notice. She knew the look in his eyes.

"Not one that concerns you."

"That's where you're wrong, friend. This is my home, and more importantly, this is my little sister. So, I suggest you lower your voice when you speak to her. I don't give a rat's ass who your daddy is. Am I making myself clear?"

Krysta couldn't take the fighting anymore. She needed some fresh air. She walked out onto the front porch without waiting to hear Bentley's reply. The cool November air took some of the steam out of her. She took a deep breath and let it out slowly. What the hell was

Kasper thinking? He had this wonderful and horrible habit of getting up in her space whenever he felt it necessary. Now she had to explain to Bentley the past she kept trying to put to rest.

Krysta heard the screen door open behind her. Without looking back, she started down the porch steps. She wasn't talking to either one of those guys. It was a female voice calling after her. She turned her head to find Sloane hurrying toward her. Krysta continued walking toward her car on the street, only she stopped at the edge of the sidewalk.

She blew out a deep breath and turned around as she waited for Sloane to reach her. This wasn't Sloane's doing. There was no reason to be rude to her friend.

Sloane smiled. It wasn't a happy smile. More like a mother who's about to prove a point to her teenage daughter. "What are you doing, Krysta?"

"I'm getting some air."

"Does he know?"

Krysta could feel the annoyance bubbling up inside her. "Know what? That I'm outside?"

"That you love him?"

"I don't."

"There's no need to pretend with me. I'm not blind."

"Bentley asked me to marry him. He's a good man and I care about him. I could do worse."

"That doesn't mean that you don't love Kasper. I see the way you look at him. There can't be that much hate without an equal amount of love."

"That was a long time ago."

"When I asked if he knew you loved him, you knew exactly who I was talking about without me saying his name. Did you even realize that? You knew I meant

Kasper and not Bentley. The heart knows no time limit. Trust me."

Krysta looked down at her feet as she tried to fight off the tears threatening to fall for the second time today. Sloane had fought her feelings for Max in the beginning. She even tried to hide the fact she was carrying his child for months. If anyone knew how Krysta was feeling, it would be Sloane. Should she admit Kasper still held a part of her heart hostage? Maybe even all of it? She didn't want to admit it, but she couldn't keep fighting it either.

"What should I do? Risk a good stable life for something that could potentially crush me yet again?"

"I'll tell you what you shouldn't do," Sloane put her hands on her hips, "you shouldn't marry a safe man you're not in love with."

"Safe?"

"Your heart is safe, Krys. You may be thinking you'll grow to love him, or mutual respect is enough. It's not. Not for you and certainly not for him. It's not fair to keep him from finding his match either."

Krysta threw her head back. Staring at the sky she let out a deep breath. "Damn you."

Sloane giggled.

"Come on in. Let's go finish getting dinner ready. I'm starving." Sloane linked their arms. They walked into the house together. The kitchen was empty now. She was thankful for the reprieve. She went back to cooking. If everything was timed properly, dinner would be ready withing the next twenty minutes. It was a good thing. She was getting hungry too. Cori came in, handing her a glass of wine.

"How did you know?"

"I knew I would want one in your shoes." Cori chuckled.

Krysta downed half the glass in one shot. The ripe, sweet taste danced on her tongue.

"Thank you."

"You know we all just want you happy, right?"

"Yeah, I do," she whispered, unable to meet her gaze.

"That's all I'm going to say about it."

Cori kissed her cheek. The timer for the oven beeped loudly. "About time. I'm starved." Cori smiled, handing her the potholders. The oven door opened, revealing a perfectly browned turkey. Krysta's stomach growled. She thought twice about pulling that bird out on her own.

"Pax," she called out. "Come help me."

"He's talking to your boyfriend. Or should I say fiancé?" Kasper's deep accusing voice startled her. When she didn't answer him, he continued. "What can I do for you?"

She glanced over her shoulder. He stood with his hands in his pockets.

"You can pull a turkey out of the oven."

"I can do that."

Kasper pulled his hands free of his pockets, taking a set of mitts from her. He leaned into the open oven and extracted the large metal roaster and placed it on the stove top.

"Thank you"

"Is there anything else I can do?"

"If you could carve it, that would be great."

He removed the turkey with two large forks and put it onto a large wooden cutting board she had waiting on the kitchen counter. Reaching over for the electric knife, he began to carve it as Krysta moved around him to get a serving platter. She set the platter next to him.

"Thank you again."

"Anything for you, Kitten." He sounded so fucking sincere her stomach clenched.

That goddamn nickname. She both hated and loved it at the same time. She loved that she was the only one he ever called that. It was her name. It wasn't interchangeable with other women. And there had been a lot of women. And yet she hated it, for reminding her of everything they once had. For reminding her of everything she would never have again.

Krysta picked up the platter, making her way through the kitchen door. She set the platter on the table and took a deep breath. "Come eat."

SIX
KASPER

KASPER FOLLOWED Krysta out of the kitchen with his eyes glued to her ass. In fact, he was so entranced by the sway of her hips he almost slammed right into the back of her when she stopped to put food on the table. He wasn't sure how long he could go on pretending there was nothing between them. She could deny it all she wanted to, but Kasper could feel it in his bones. He could see it in her eyes when he rolled his sleeves up. He knew exactly what that did to her. Once he overheard her talking to one of her friends about it, he did it frequently just to turn her on when he came to hang out with Tank. He would be surprised if their friends hadn't figured out something was brewing by now.

He sat down across the table from her so he could watch her beautiful face as she laughed and carried on animatedly in conversations around the table. He forgot her stupid boyfriend was here. *Fiancé. Was she really gonna marry this guy*? She wasn't wearing a ring. He sat down next to her, where Kasper should have been. Maybe it was time to rile his little kitten up again.

"So what do you do for a living, Lexus?"

"Bentley," the guy chastised.

"Yeah, that's what I said."

"I'm a corporate attorney. However, I plan to run for state governor next year."

Krysta looked surprised. "You are? You must have failed to mention it to me."

"I was going to at dinner later with my parents."

"I wasn't going to be at dinner tonight."

"That's why I'm here, to rectify that."

Kasper watched as she cast her gaze down on her plate. She pushed her food around, nibbling on her lower lip. Something was on her mind, he would give anything to know what that was. He used to be able to read her so well. Her face had always shown her emotions as clearly as if she'd said them out loud. That was until that night. That fucked up night she walked away from him in the dark alone. And he let her. He fucking let her walk away. She looked up, her eyes meeting his. Was that sadness in her eyes?

"Good luck." Marabella smiled sweetly.

More of the same came from everyone else at the table. Tank however, had a watchful eye on his baby sister. Kasper leaned back in his seat.

"Public officials deal with a lot of shit. Nothing stays hidden when the vultures come sniffin' around. Right, Jaguar? Got any skeletons we'll be able to read about?" Kasper pushed, waggling his eyebrows, pasting a huge fake smile on his face.

"Lexus. Jaguar. It wasn't funny the first time, nor is it now. I think it's time we get going." Bentley turned to Cori, effectively ignoring his question. Krysta's eyes practically bugged out of her head. "Thank you for dinner, Tori."

Tori?

"Jesus fuck. It's Cori, for the millionth time," Krysta growled. "We just sat down to eat. What the hell?"

Cori bit her lip before covering her mouth with her hand. Tank sat up straighter in his chair.

"Krys. Seriously? You know how I feel about that."

Krysta was turning red right before Kasper's eyes. It started on her chest and quickly moved up her neck to her cheeks. He wouldn't have been surprised if she passed out from how fast her blood pressure was rising. He didn't understand what the fuck was going on, but he knew it was about to get good.

Her eyes landed on Kasper again. He gave her what he hoped was his best smirk followed by a wink. Her eyes hardened, enraging her even more. *There she was.* Here we go, dinner and a show.

"Bentley, do not talk to me like a fucking child."

"We should discuss this in private."

"No need on our account, dude. You put your foot in it this time. Might as well air it out."

"Fuck you, Kass," she bit out.

"That's my girl." *Shit.* He didn't mean to say that part out loud.

Bentley looked back and forth between the two of them. It would have been comical if not for the daggers Krysta glared at him.

"I'm sorry, what?" Bentley knew exactly what he let slip. It was too fucking late now.

"Ignore him, he's an assfuck," she growled.

No lie, she fucking growled at him. Damn, she was hot.

He could make a comment about him fucking her ass, but Tank would rip his nuts off, and he was quite attached to them. So for once he kept his big mouth closed. Kasper spread his legs some in his seat to make room for the growing bulge in his pants just from the image that thought conjured. Thank God for the long tablecloth.

"Krysta." Tank finally stood up.

"I'm fine," she barked, glaring across the table.

Bentley scoffed, "Not likely."

Did this man have a death wish? Kasper had witnessed her tear men down with her words in the past. It was hilarious as long as you weren't the poor slob on the receiving end. He had been on more than one occasion. Swinging to face him, she put a hand on her hip.

"You, outside. Right the *fuck* now." She enunciated the word fuck.

She stormed out of the room without a backward glance. You could hear a pin drop in the room until the front door slammed.

"I do not envy you, friend." Max let loose a long whistle.

Sloane elbowed him in his ribs. "Stop instigating."

"Me? Gutter was the instigator. I was simply making a statement."

"My sister is a bit volatile when people tell her what to do, haven't you realized that yet?" Tank chuckled.

"No." Bentley stood, bushing his hands down his slacks. "She's usually more…reserved."

"Seriously?" Sloane blinked rapidly in confusion.

"You seem surprised."

"We are." Bella giggled. "She's usually quite…what's the word I'm looking for?"

"Opinionated?" Sloane smiled.

"Bossy?" Foster added.

"Stubborn?" Tank laughed.

Beautiful. Wild. Fucking amazing, he thought.

Krysta stormed back in, placed her hands on her hips, and glared at Bentley. "I'm fucking waiting," she all but yelled across the room.

"Excuse me, everyone." Bentley left the table to follow Krysta back the way she came.

"They seem like an odd couple," Marabella whispered, slowly standing. She placed her hand on her large belly as she backed away from the table, scurrying off without another word.

Foster watched her go before turning back to the group. "She always has to pee."

Sloane slipped from her seat. "I'm gonna go check on the kids." She pointed at Max. "Behave."

Max rolled his eyes with a playful smile, gifting his woman a smack on the ass as she walked off to check on the napping toddlers. Conversation continued around the table. He didn't even bother to pretend to listen to any of them. He was too busy wondering if it would be odd if he went to check on Krysta.

Tank put his hand on his shoulder. Kasper didn't realize he'd moved as if to stand. He looked at his best friend.

"She's fine." Tank nodded in the direction of his sister. Why was Tank looking at him like that?

"Of course she is." Kasper shook his comment off, shrugging as he leaned back in his chair once again.

He itched to go to her, though. He wanted to wrap her in his arms and promise she'd never hurt again. He knew that was ridiculous. He could no more guarantee that than he could guarantee a winning lottery ticket. She wouldn't believe him even if he did. He'd already hurt her once. Bella and Sloane came around the corner, both of them carrying a sleepy child in their arms. *The next generation*, he thought.

He could have had that if he hadn't pushed her away. *If he hadn't pushed her to…* He couldn't even think about that. They weren't ready. He knew that. He still told himself he wasn't going to father kids, up until Raelyn was born. Being "Uncle Kass" made him realize what he was missing.

Krysta entered the house with Richie Rich on her tail. She took a seat, plucking her wine glass off the table. She gulped the red liquid down until the glass was empty. Her cheeks pinked up as they always did when she drank. Kasper wasn't sure if maybe he'd drank too much. *Did she just wink at him? What the fuck?*

"Cori, thank you for a lovely dinner." *One he didn't bother to eat.*

"Leaving so soon?" Tank asked.

"I have to get going, my parents are expecting me. It was nice meeting all of you"

He looked down at Krysta one more time before walking out of the house. Interesting.

Krysta tucked into her food along with everyone else at the table beside him and Tank.

"What the fu-fudge"—Tank eyed the toddlers—"just happened?"

Krysta shrugged. "Nothing. So, I was thinking I'd stay for a few more days, if that's okay with you."

"Since when do you ask?"

"I'm being polite, lint licker."

She used the insult she called him when she was a kid. The whole table chuckled. Kasper couldn't hide his smile. There was a fire in her even back then. Just like that, everything went back to normal. It was as if the boyfriend had never been here at all. Kasper was more than happy for that.

SEVEN
KRYSTA

THERE, she did it. She told Bentley it wasn't going to work between the two of them. Her timing probably sucked, however. When he called Cori by the wrong name again, something in her snapped—especially after he'd corrected Kasper so vehemently. Kasper was just being a dick, as usual. She realized she'd never fit into the mold Bentley envisioned for her. It had nothing to do with the man currently sitting across from her—at least that's what she told herself.

Getting up, she took hers and Bentley's plates to the kitchen. The countertops were piled with extra food and dirty dishes. Someone needed to clean up, and she needed a reprieve from being the evening's entertainment, so she rolled up her sleeves and got to work. She was loading the dishwasher with the silverware as she thought about this evening.

All her interactions with Kasper seemed odd today. The day started as usual. He was a dick and she made sure he knew it. Then she saw pieces of the Kasper she fell in love with. The way he looked at her from across the room or the way he spoke low and sexy in her ear. He had a possessiveness in his voice once Bentley arrived. Now, Kasper was quieter than usual. She wondered what that was all about.

She didn't know what to make of him lately.

"You gonna tell us what went down outside?" her big brother questioned, breaking through her thoughts.

She was so lost in her own head she didn't even hear Paxton enter the room. She grabbed a hand towel to dry her hands off. Turning round, she leaned against the sink, tossing the towel on the counter behind her.

"I wasn't planning on it." She grinned.

"Krysta…" His voice dropped off. He grabbed a beer from the fridge, twisting the cap off. He didn't take a drink though. He set it on the counter, leaning forward with his elbows resting on each side of the bottle, staring at her. She knew that look. She wasn't gonna get him off her back unless she told him something.

"Fine, it's done. I broke off the engagement. There were a lot of reasons, none of which I would like to discuss with you right now."

"Okay." He stood up straight. Picking up his beer, he finally took a swig.

"You aren't gonna fight me on this? You're just gonna let it go?" She scowled at him. *What was his angle?*

"Did he hurt you?"

"No. God, no, Pax. I'd never keep something like that from you."

"Then yes, I'm gonna let it go. If and when you wanna talk about it, I'm here for you."

Closing the distance between them, Krysta threw her arms around Paxton's neck. "Thank you," she whispered before taking a step back.

"You don't have to do these right now." He gestured to the dishes. "I'll do them later."

"I don't mind. I need a few minutes to myself anyway. This is a good excuse."

He nodded in understanding before cupping the back of her head. He kissed her forehead like their parents always did, then left her alone.

Taking a deep cleansing breath, she turned around to tackle the dishes once again. Cori brought in more, setting them on the island silently before she dipped back out to join everyone. Marabella and Foster popped in to hug her goodbye. Marabella was exhausted and they wanted to get Seth put to bed. Max and Sloane were only a few minutes behind them.

"Remember what I said," Sloane murmured in her ear during the hug.

Krysta squeezed her tighter. "I will. Thank you."

Max lifted her off the ground with a bear hug as she erupted with laughter.

"He wasn't the one, Krys. Don't let it worry you."

"I think you might be right. Drive safe. Love you both."

Krysta appreciated the quiet time, but she knew she couldn't hide out in here forever. She grabbed a glass of wine, joining Paxton, Cori, and Kasper where they all sat around the fire pit in the backyard, laughing. It was a gorgeous evening even if it was a bit chilly. Kasper appeared beside her with a blanket, holding it out to her.

"Thank you," she whispered.

She wrapped the blanket around her legs. Her shoulders were still a little cold, but at least she could put her arms partially under the blanket.

"May I?"

He pointed to the spot next to her on the bench. She wanted to tell him she did mind, but then he would know how much he still affected her. It was getting harder to deny it, even to herself. She nodded to the space instead. Kasper sat down next to her with his own blanket. Instead of putting it on his lap, he put half over her shoulder, the other across his own on the opposite side. They were practically hip to hip. Without thinking, she readjusted her blanket to cover both their legs.

In this blanket, cocooned with Kasper, his scent was overwhelming. Krysta didn't even need to breathe in to smell him. His intoxicating scent teased her mind with memories of them wrapped up together in their spot overlooking the town. The best times of her life happened there. Until that last time.

"Thanks for sharing." He motioned to the blanket now covering his lap.

Krysta looked across the fire. Paxton and Cori were cuddled up in their blankets, only their arms were around each other. They stole sweet kisses during breaks in the conversation. She wanted that. She wanted to be loved that way. She'd never been the priority to anyone. She was always second place. Whether it was to a career, another girl, or even a best friend. Krysta didn't know what it felt like to be the sun to someone.

She was so fucking happy for her brother. She knew someday he'd fall in love again. He had a big heart, and it was bound to meet its match. Cori was everything she'd hoped he'd find. That didn't mean she wanted to sit here and watch them kissing and giggling while she sat next to Kasper. Lost in thought, she startled when his hand slipped in hers under the blanket. He squeezed it lightly. Krysta looked up into Kasper's eyes. He wanted to say something. She could read it in those mesmerizing orbs.

His eyes flicked to her lips for a moment. *Did he want to kiss her? In front of Paxton? What the fuck is he thinking? He couldn't. It would ruin his friendship.* Her heart sped up, pounding in her chest. Fuck, it got hot all of a sudden. Kasper's finger trailed to her wrist, a slow smile tugged at the corner of his mouth. The smug bastard had his finger on her pulse point. He knew exactly what he did to her.

Pulling her hand away from him, she stood up. "I'm wiped out. It's been a long ass day. I'm gonna head to bed."

"Need someone to tuck you in, Kitten?"

Kasper waggled his eyes like a cartoon character. Paxton laughed. She held her middle finger up as she sauntered back into the house. He thought he was so fucking smart. Stopping in the kitchen, she put her glass in the dishwasher. Once in her room, she dug some clothes from her bag. Slipping on a satin tank top and matching shorts, she crawled into bed. She would not lay here thinking about a certain smug shithead.

EIGHT
KASPER

THE COUCH WASN'T AS bad as Kasper thought it would be. He still couldn't fall asleep though. Two hours he lay there, replaying the evening in his mind. He wanted so badly to kiss her sitting by the fire. He didn't know if it was the proximity, the stars above, or her scent teasing his dick. Whatever it was that urged him on didn't give two shits if his best friend—her big brother—was sitting across from them.

A soft light came spilling across the floor. Slipping from the couch, he walked into the kitchen. Krysta was moving bottles of beer to the side to get to the bottles of water in the back. *Jesus, what was she wearing?* Those shorts barely covered her ass cheeks, and fuck, he could see her nipples pressing into the pale pink fabric. She cracked the bottle open, taking a long drink. He stood silently watching her. The way the tender muscles of her throat worked as she swallowed the liquid. He could imagine what it would feel like if it were his dick in her mouth.

He must've groaned out loud. Krysta whirled around,

dropping the half full bottle to the floor. Water splashed everywhere.

"Shit," she exclaimed. "What the fuck, Kass? You don't sneak up on someone in the dark like that."

"I was thirsty. I didn't realize anyone was in here," he lied, hoping like hell she didn't see through it. Or the erection he was beginning to sport. He crossed the room, grabbing the roll of paper towels. The movement afforded him a moment to adjust his hard on inconspicuously. Krysta picked the mostly empty water bottle up as he wiped the spill from the floor. Then he went to the still opened fridge to retrieve a bottle for himself. His arm brushed the side of her breast as he reached passed her, eliciting a sharp inhale of breath from her. She was going to be the death of him. It would be worth it.

Krysta stood still, watching him, her eyes dropping to his lips. He chugged the entire bottle of water in one go before crushing the plastic flat and tossing it in the trash. *Fuck it.* He cupped her face in his hands. Her tongue darted out, swiping quickly across her bottom lip. Kasper crushed his lips to hers. Her hands slid up to his. He imagined she'd pull away like she had at lunch, but she didn't. She pressed him tighter to her. He swept his tongue across her lip like she did a moment ago. Parting her lips, Krysta allowed him access to deepen their kiss. He wasn't going to let this moment get away.

He tilted her head where he wanted it and dove in headfirst. She tasted like mint toothpaste, a past he fucked up, and a future he desperately wanted. Her arms circled his neck, her body pressed into him. There was no way she didn't feel his cock demanding attention. She moved her hands down his bare chest.

Kasper couldn't hold back anymore. Removing his

hands from her face, he gripped her thighs, pulling her legs around his waist. Her arms once again circled his neck while she locked her ankles behind his back to hold on to him better. Pressing her against the side of the fridge, he ground his cock against her center. He could feel the heat coming from her pussy as she rocked her hips in time with his. Illuminated only in the fridge light, he devoured her mouth. He shut the door with his foot as he turned, plunging them in darkness, and headed for her room.

The bedroom door was still open. Once inside, he closed it the same way he did the fridge, marching straight to her bed. He set her down. He looked into her lust-filled eyes for a sign he should stop, even though that was the last fucking thing he wanted. Instead of stopping him, she pulled her satiny tank top over her head, throwing it to the floor. Something in him broke. He kissed her hard, then trailed his mouth down her chin line, to her neck, until finally he took a perfect pink nipple into his mouth. She arched into his touch.

He sucked, licked, and flicked her nipple before turning his attention to the other one. His body was on fire for her. Her scent invaded his head. It took up residence like it was there to stay. God, did he want her to stay. He resumed his path of kisses lower, dragging her barely there shorts down her soft as fuck legs. Kasper slid his tongue across her delicate folds. She was already dripping wet for him. He gripped his cock through his own shorts for a little relief. He was so hard for her it was almost painful.

He ate her pussy like a man starved. That was how he felt too. Starved for this woman. Sliding a finger into her, she practically purred. Her orgasm built as her muscles started to flutter around him. He added a second finger, pumping slowly while curling the digits to hit the perfect spot. Once, twice, three times and Krysta erupted. Squeezing his fingers so tight, he couldn't wait to feel her come on his cock. Fucking magical.

"I'm gonna fuck this beautiful cunt, Kitten. If you don't want that, you're gonna have to tell me now," he growled as he stood up to remove his shorts. He kept his fingers in the waistband, waiting for a response.

"Fuck me, Kass. Fuck me now."

Kasper didn't need to be told again. He removed his only article of clothes, then positioned himself over her. He took his cock in hand, rubbing the tip through her juices before plunging into her. Her hands splayed across his back as he continued at a punishing rhythm. *Jesus*. He needed a minute before he embarrassed himself. Pulling out of her gave a moment's reprieve and Krysta whimpered.

"Up on those knees. Let me see that gorgeous ass, baby."

Without a word she rolled over, presenting her lush ass with a playful wiggle. Kasper smacked one cheek before gripping her hips and impaling her on his cock again. She gasped, burying her face in a pillow to muffle the sounds.

He thrust himself inside her perfect wet heat, over and over again. Her inner muscles started to flutter again, and he knew she was close. Thank God, because he didn't know how much longer he could prolong this. He felt the familiar sensation starting in his balls, his cock swelling, ready to release. He slapped her other ass cheek. Her moans just about killed him.

"Fuck. So close, Kasper," she purred.

"That's it. Say my fucking name. Come for me, Kitten."

Kasper reached around, pinching her clit the way she'd liked in the past.

"Kasper!" Her repressed cry pushed him past the point of no return.

She came so hard her pussy strangled his cock. Her continued screams of his name were muffled by the pillow she clung to. It was so fucking perfect, he couldn't form a complete thought. He roared his release into her neck. She shivered beneath him as ropes of hot cum left his body, each one more intense than the last.

He couldn't move. Didn't want to move. Being inside of her was too fucking good. He could feel their combined release running down his balls. That's when he realized what he'd done.

"Fuck!" He pulled out of her slowly. The caveman part of him thought it was hot as fuck to watch his cum slowly drip from between her swollen pussy lips. Okay, so it was all of him, not just the caveman part.

"What's wrong?" She looked over her shoulder at him. Her cheeks were flushed. She was magnificent. He'd never believed he would get another chance to see her sated like this. Only here she was, and he fucked up again. He never went without a condom. That was his number one rule.

"I took you raw. I didn't even remember to pull out. I'm so sorry. Fuck!" He speared his fingers through his hair.

"It's…okay. I'm on the pill." She lowered herself to the bed, rolling over to face him.

"I'm clean. I was tested a few weeks ago. I haven't been with anyone since."

Surprise fluttered across her face for the briefest moment.

"Are you surprised?" he asked.

"It's unusual for you. That's all."

Krysta plucked a robe off the chair beside the bed, covering her gorgeous body. Her remark shouldn't have mattered, but it did. Contrary to his past actions, he wasn't some animal that had to fuck everything that moved.

"I do know how to control myself," he retorted irritably.

"Obviously." Krysta rolled her eyes. "I need to go clean up. You should go back to the couch, so Paxton doesn't find out about this." She waved her arms between the two of them.

Krysta moved past him quickly, out of her room and across the hall, shutting the bathroom door behind her. Kasper stood frozen until the sound of the shower snapped him out of it.

NINE
KRYSTA

HOLY FUCK, she kept repeating in her head as the hot water beat against her skin. She swore she wouldn't fall back into the trap that was Kasper Guttenmuth. Yet here she was, standing in the shower with his cum running down her legs. The worst part was how much she'd wanted him. How much she still did even now. He was a danger to her heart.

She poured soap on a loofa. Once it was sudsy, she began scrubbing her body down, the scent of her lavender vanilla soap was doing nothing to calm her like it usually did. At least it removed his scent from her skin. When the hot water turned tepid, she got out of the shower. Her skin was red and angry from all the scrubbing. Wrapping the robe around herself once again, she scurried back to her room.

She was relieved to find the room empty. Or was she? She was equal parts relieved and disappointed. What the hell was wrong with her? Flopping onto the bed, she pulled the sheet over her body, not bothering with clothes. She needed to get her head on straight—starting with her living arrangements. She needed to get her things from Bentley's place. She knew she could stay here as long as she wanted, but she didn't want to put out Paxton and Cori any more than she already had. Krysta resolved to figure it out first thing tomorrow. For now she needed sleep.

———

Krysta peeled her eyes open to the smell of coffee and bacon. She tossed on a clean tank top and cotton shorts before hustling to the kitchen. Paxton was removing bacon from the oven. Her mouth started to water. Cori looked up from where she was pouring a cup of coffee. She set it in front of Krysta.

"Eggs will be done in just a minute." She winked.

Why did she wink? Do they know? Krysta poured creamer into the mug. "Sounds good. I'm starving."

"Bad dreams last night?" Paxton asked around a mouthful of bacon.

"No, actually. Why?"

"Just thought I heard a few moans at one point. I almost came to check on you, but I didn't want to startle you and make it worse."

Just lovely. My brother no doubt heard me orgasm last night and now he was worried about me. He should be. I was a complete moron. "I guess I did, I don't remember. Sorry if I woke you."

Paxton's gaze landed over her shoulder. Even if he hadn't noticed the movement, she would have known Kasper entered the room. The energy was different when he was around. Like a tuning fork, her body responded. It was even worse this morning. No doubt it had to do with how in tune they had been last night. Her body heated up and her thighs squeezed together of their own accord at the delicious memory.

"Smells amazing in here." He scratched his hands through his hair, the long strands slipping through his fingers.

Kasper was wearing the same shorts as last night. His hair was tousled, and she couldn't help but want him all over again. Why did he have to be so fucking gorgeous? At least he added a shirt before entering the kitchen this time. His gaze raked over her. The corner of his lip quirked up in a secretive grin. She rolled her eyes at him.

"So, I was thinking about moving back this way," she announced, taking a sip of coffee.

Everyone's head whipped her way. Paxton's smile was brilliant. It made her belly warm with even more love for her brother.

"Really?"

"Yeah, I mean, why not? I don't have anything worth going back to. I can work anywhere, and I've been thinking about it a lot actually." She shrugged like it was no big deal. "I don't want to be all up in your space all the time."

"Like Kasper?" Cori gave him a pretend glare before smiling at him.

"Maybe the big guy here likes it, Doc. If he didn't, he'd make sure the door was locked before he went muff diving."

"You two are gonna be the death of me." She turned back to Krysta. "What can we do to help?"

There was the million-dollar question.

"I'll need a place of my own, don't suppose I could stay at your old place next door?" she asked, a hopefulness in her voice. "I know you have it up for sale right now."

"You would want to?" Tank asked as Cori raised an eyebrow.

Krysta crossed her arms over her chest. "It's just a house, right? If I'm really going to put the past behind me, maybe it's the best place to do it. Plus, I like the idea of being next door to you guys." In reality, she was a little worried. She killed a man in that house. Put a bullet right in his head to save the people she loved. She would do it again, too.

"I like it, too," Tank admitted. "I just don't want you doing more harm than good being there alone at night."

"I'll stay with her," Kasper mumbled around a mouthful of eggs.

"Say what?" Krysta could feel her eyes grow wide in confusion.

He shrugged like he didn't just offer to invade her space for an undetermined amount of time. Could she be around him alone and not want to rip his clothes off? No. The answer was a resounding no. Maybe that wouldn't be so bad. A few days to get Kasper naked and work him out of her system once and for all. No one else would be the wiser.

"I'll stay there if it'll help."

"Dude, that sounds like…a disaster," Paxton scoffed.

"That's actually a great idea," Cori interjected. "Having him there will be an added assurance that she's safe. It'll hopefully keep away any panic attacks, and if she does have one, Kass can help walk her though it."

Kasper tossed his paper plate in the trash. He dropped his fork into the dishwasher and leaned against the sink, nodding his agreement. "Whaddya think, Kitten? Wanna playhouse with me?" He winked.

"God, I can't believe I'm considering this," she lied. Blowing out a breath, she dragged her hand through her long tresses. She looked Kasper in the eyes. "I wouldn't say no to you staying in the guest room to make sure I don't lose my shit for a few days. I have to get my stuff from Bentley's."

"It's settled then. I'll take my bike home, get my truck, and grab some clothes and stuff."

"I probably won't be back tonight."

"Why not?" His brows furrowed.

"I have to rent a truck, load everything in it, and pack my stuff. That takes time."

"Okay, new plan. Ride back with me. We'll take my truck, hitch a trailer to it, and be outta there in half the time." He smirked at her.

"All right. Remember, you offered."

"Dumbass." Paxton laughed.

Cori smacked his arm playfully. "Just for that comment, you can help me go air the place out a bit. I'm sure it needs a good dusting after all this time."

"Dust what? There's no furniture over there."

The look of confusion was priceless. Paxton put his hands on his hips, creating the illusion he was bigger and broader than he already was. He wasn't nicknamed Tank for nothing. Cori wasn't intimidated in the least. She mimicked his posture without saying a word.

Paxton turned to Krysta. "So Cori and I are gonna go air out the house and make sure it's cleaned up for you."

"What a bitch." Kasper laughed.

Krysta moved around the island to hug her brother. She kissed his cheek. "Thanks, Pax."

"Get moving. You're burnin' daylight."

Their father used to say that all the time. Whenever he was waiting on them or their mother. He would call up the stairs, "We're burnin' daylight here. Move your ass." She still missed them every day.

She turned to find Kasper watching her. He had been around enough growing up, she knew he understood the reference. "I'm gonna change really quick."

TEN
KASPER

KASPER WASN'T sure what surprised him more; the fact he offered to stay with her, or that she actually accepted. He wanted an excuse to be around her. He wanted to talk to Tank too, but that wasn't going to happen right now. Now he had to go get her stuff from that guy's place. There was no way he was going to let her go alone. What if he was there and tried to change her mind about their relationship? Kasper couldn't chance that. He'd had another taste of her. He would do what he needed in order to keep her.

Getting to spend even more time with her wouldn't be a hardship, either. If she thought he was just sleeping there for a few days, she was mistaken. He was moving in. She just didn't know it yet. He had plans to make Krysta Sokolofski his forever. He swapped his shorts for a pair of jeans. He'd just put the shirt on clean this morning. He walked out of the bathroom the same time Krysta exited the bedroom she'd been using, almost colliding.

She was fucking breathtaking. Clean faced, a ponytail keeping her long locks pulled back, dressed in a Mayday

Parade long sleeve tee. The kind that sits just about her waist, so anytime she moves her arms there's a peek of skin. Like a siren song, that sliver of skin could lead a man to his death. He wanted to suck that tender skin into his mouth, hard. Mark her perfect flesh. Which was ridiculous. He was a grown ass man. He hadn't given a girl a hickey in years. He wanted to right this minute, nonetheless.

He cleared his throat. "Got a coat?"

It was sixty degrees outside. Warm for the end of November. However, on the bike, the wind would cut through her shirt like a warm knife through butter.

"Right. I forgot." She waved absentmindedly as she disappeared back into the room, reemerging with a medium weight jacket. At least the ride to his apartment was a short one. After that, she'd be in the warmth of his truck.

"Leaving," she yelled to Tank as she strode out the front door.

He followed behind her, trying and failing not to stare at her perfect ass. The very one he had his hands all over less than ten hours ago. She stopped in front of his baby. Opening his saddlebag, he removed his helmet, propping it on top of the seat before reaching back in the bag for his spare. He held it out to her.

She held it in her hands, eyes glued to it as if it were a foreign object she'd never seen before.

"What is it?" he asked.

"I haven't..." She trailed off for a moment. Taking a fortifying inhale, she let it out slowly. "I haven't been on a bike since you," she whispered conspiratorially, throwing a look over her shoulder.

Obviously, she was worried her brother would overhear from inside the house. It was ridiculous for him to feel hurt she was worried about Tank finding out. To feel like a dirty secret since it was his doing to begin with. He wanted to keep their relationship from Tank, from the world.

For the entire time they were seeing each other he came up with excuse after excuse after excuse as to why they should wait just a little bit longer. Now, he would yell it from the rooftops if she'd have him. Did she think last night was a one-time thing? He would need to set the record straight on that.

He threw a leg over the side of the bike, patting the seat behind him with a wink. "Well, come on. Time to reacquaint the two of you."

Krysta situated herself behind him. She tried to sit back on the bike seat as far as she could and still hold on to his shoulders. There was no way she had forgotten how to ride, so the only conclusion was she wanted to touch him as little as possible. That simply wouldn't do. Not one fucking bit.

"Come on now, Kitten. Don't be shy." He took her hand from his shoulder, wrapping it around his chest. Placing it over his heart. She was tentative at first. Barely applying any pressure. As he used his feet to back them down the drive, he wanted to get her used to the feel of the bike again. She wrapped her arms around his midsection.

The heat from her body pressed against him made his dick perk up. He didn't realize how much he had missed her riding with him until just now. She felt right. She belonged there.

The ride to his apartment went faster than he would have liked. He should have gone the long way to keep her plastered to him a little longer. Unfortunately, they had things to do. *There would be other times,* he told himself.

"So was it everything you remembered?" he joked. Mostly.

"I forgot how freeing it was." She cast her eyes downward. Was she lost in thought or avoiding eye contact?

"Come on up. Let me snag some clothes really quick and we'll be on our way."

Krysta followed him to his second-floor apartment. Unlocking the door, he ushered her in before him. His place was nothing special. Through the door was an open space. The living area to the left. The kitchen to the right. He usually ate in front of the television or at the island, so he never bothered with a dining table. It was sparsely decorated, but what he did have was high quality. His apartment was small, so he really didn't need much. He spent most of his time at work or with Tank at his house. Krysta's eyes darted everywhere, taking it all in.

"It's nice."

"It's pretty small, but I don't need much."

"Still bigger than what I had before I move in with Bentley."

Bentley. It took everything he had not to roll his eyes at her ex-boyfriend's name. He still couldn't believe she moved in with a guy like that. Much less got engaged. *She was really gonna marry that guy?*

"Make yourself at home. I'll only be a few minutes."

Marching to his room at the end of the hall, he grabbed an extra-large duffle from the back of his closet. He packed enough clothes for a week. Moving to the bathroom, he filled his toiletry bag. He tossed it into the duffle as well. Anything else he needed he could swing by and get. He had the essentials.

Krysta was sitting on his couch. Her head leaned back, eyes closed. Was she sleeping? He hated to wake her if she was. He also didn't want to delay their departure. He hoped to get her stuff loaded before they could be

interrupted. He set his bag down by the door, swiping a bottle of cold water from the fridge. He thought about last night. They were perfect together, explosive even.

"Can I get one of those for the road?" she asked, eyes still closed

"Sure thing." He retrieved another bottle. You ready to hit the road?"

"Absolutely." She sat up. "This couch is amazing."

She stood, stretching her body up on her toes. He watched her every move.

"My favorite thing about my whole place. I think I fall asleep there more than I do the bedroom." He smiled.

He wasn't sure why it made him happy she liked his couch. It just did. Kasper met her at the front door, extending the bottle to her. She took it, her eyes on both their hands gripping the bottle. A smile tugged her full lips before stepping back. Was she remembering it too?

He followed her out, his bag now thrown over his shoulder. Once they were in the truck, he turned the key in the ignition, glancing at her as the truck roared to life.

"Enough burnin' daylight. Let's get this show started."

She kept her eyes focused on the windshield, but a smile curled her lips. It was a beautiful start.

ELEVEN
KRYSTA

THE DRIVE to Bentley's place went faster than she thought it would. The conversation between them flowed smoothly, in fact, they talked about work, Paxton and Cori, and how she was coping with what she did. Kasper understood in a way Bentley never had. Bentley always wanted her to forget and pretend it never happened, whereas Kasper wanted to hear every detail she was willing to relive. It was hard at first, but by the end of the ride it had been cathartic.

She'd never opened up much to her brother or Cori. They were too close to it. She knew Paxton felt like a failure for a while since he couldn't save her on his own, he felt like it was his duty. He loathed the fact that Krysta had to be the one to pull that trigger.

"There's no timeline to get over something like this, Kitten."

"Thank you for that." She meant it, too.

Entering the apartment, Krysta turned to Kasper to grab one of the cardboard boxes they'd picked up with the trailer. She was studying the space much like she did this morning.

"You live here?" His eyes quirked up.

"I did," she replied defensively.

"It wasn't my intention to sound like an ass. I just mean, I don't see anything here that says you live here. That's all."

"My stuff clashed with Bentley's style. It's not a big deal. I kept the important stuff. It's back here. A lot of it is still packed in boxes in the closet in here."

Kasper followed her down the hall. The spare bedroom wasn't big. It had enough space for her bed—the frame had belonged to her parents—and her desk.

"Everything in here goes. I'll pack up what's in the master bedroom."

"Let me know if you need me to carry anything."

With her suitcase open on the bed in the master bedroom, Krysta began filling it quickly. She wanted to get out of there before Bentley came home. Since it was the day after Thanksgiving, he could be home at any time. She didn't want to push her luck.

"Kitten. Do you have a Phillips head screwdriver? I didn't think to bring one. Dumb, I know." He admonished himself with a chuckle.

"Yeah." She pulled a small bag from the inside of the walk-in closet, pilfering a screwdriver. She handed it over. Their fingers touched and she felt fire spread over her body.

"Thanks." He winked.

That shouldn't give her butterflies, but it did. He just had that way about him. As much as she tried, she was helpless against how he made her feel. Before last night, she'd at least been able to pretend her heart didn't leap whenever he was near. She could pretend she could erase the years since that heartbreaking night years ago. She could pretend, but it was useless. Her body remembered all the delicious things he could do to it. And yet her heart remembered too. Remembered the agonizing pain he put it through.

She couldn't go through that again. Her fragile heart couldn't survive it. She straightened her shoulders. She had to let it go. After this week, she'd have him out of her system, one way or another.

The trailer was loaded with all her belongings from the spare room by the time she finished up in the master. Taking a key from her key ring, she left it and her engagement ring on the kitchen island where Bentley would be sure to see it. She blew out a breath, rubbed her hand cross the back of her neck, straightened her shoulders, and said with as much gusto as she could, "Let's go home."

Kasper surprised her once again, this time throwing his arm around her shoulders. "That's got a nice ring to it, Kitten." He waggled his eyebrows at her.

"There's something wrong with you." She laughed out loud.

"No doubt." He gave her a wicked grin. Once outside, he opened the passenger door for her, then jogged around, hopping in the driver's seat.

"Thanks a lot for everything. You're a pretty good friend when you're not being a raging asshole." She smirked.

TWELVE
KASPER

FRIEND.

Friend.

Friend. Kasper played her words on a loop in his head the entire drive home. He didn't wanna be her friend anymore. No, that wasn't right. He didn't want to be just her friend. He wanted to be her future. Her everything. The way she was for him.

How? Well, that was the ten billion dollar question, wasn't it? He knew she wanted him physically. That much was abundantly clear. The way her body still responded to him was electrifying. It was a heady feeling to know he could still work her into a frenzy.

Easing into the driveway at Cori's house, Kasper trotted across the lawn to Tank's front door. He tried the knob, it was unlocked. Grinning, he walked inside.

"If you're fucking, just yell where the house keys are," he called out.

Cori walked in from the kitchen with a look of disappointment on her face, shaking her head.

"Hey there, beautiful. Got keys for next door?"

She didn't make a move. She stood there examining him. It wasn't how most women sized him up. There was nothing sexual or heated in her gaze. It was all clinical. Like a scientist watching the animals in the zoo.

"What's up, Doc?"

At that she laughed, caught off guard. "I was just wondering why you volunteered your services so quickly today."

"Krys is Tank's baby sister. I grew up with them. Why wouldn't I help my best friend have a little peace of mind where his sister was concerned?"

It was at that moment he realized she knew something was up. Maybe not the whole story, but the Doc knew something.

"Don't insult my intelligence, Kass."

"What do you want me to say?" He threw his hands in the air. He'd never spoken about his feelings toward Krysta. Never. "I'm head over fucking heels for my best friend's baby sister. How's that? Makes me sound like scum, doesn't it?"

"First off, it makes you sound human. Secondly, she's not a kid, Kasper. Krysta is a grown woman."

"I know. Fuck, do I know." He paced the living room, spearing his hands into his hair.

"Ohhh…" Cori wore the surprise all over her face.

He let his head fall back. Taking a deep breath, he looked into Cori's eyes, pleading with her without saying word.

"She's out there waiting for me. Can we keep this between us for now? Please?"

She opened a drawer on the end table next to the couch, retrieving a keychain with a single key. She held out the ring but pulled it away just as his fingers touched the metal.

"Give me a dollar."

"You're charging me for your house keys?" he asked incredulously.

"Just give me a dollar. Fucking men. Can't just listen, always have to ask questions," she mumbled as he produced a five dollar bill from his wallet, holding it out to her.

"Only got a five."

"That'll do." She handed over the key. "Doctor-patient confidentiality. You just paid for my services. Your secret is safe with me." She smiled smugly.

"Thanks, Doc." He grinned.

Turning, he left the house, jumping down all the steps out front. He sprinted to Krysta. She was still sitting in the truck, out of the cold. He jiggled the key at eye level. She opened the truck door and joined him walking up the steps to Cori's house.

"I thought maybe you walked in on them, and Cori finally killed you."

"You aren't that lucky, Kitten."

"I don't want you to die, Kass. Just get your ass beat a time or two." She laughed, and it was magical.

It was a laugh he remembered growing up with. The bratty little girl who turned into an amazing woman. He was helpless. There was no way he could have gone through life without falling in love with this creature.

Kasper laughed along with her. Unlocking the door, he walked inside. It was abundantly clear there was zero furniture in the house. Well, this evening just got more interesting.

THIRTEEN
KRYSTA

THEY CARRIED everything into the house. The empty house. How did she not anticipate this? She knew the house was for sale. She'd just assumed it would be staged for buyers. She knew better than to assume.

"I'm starving. Pizza? Carlito's?" Kasper asked.

"Mmmmm, Carlito's pizza is orgasmic," she agreed enthusiastically.

"A dozen pizza pies coming right up," he joked.

"Works?"

"Of course."

She called to place their order as Kasper headed upstairs.

"About thirty minutes," she yelled as she made her way up the stairs.

She stopped in the doorway, watching as Kasper put the frame of her bed together. The last time she was in this doorway she killed a man. Fucking hell. Could she really sleep in here now? She chewed her bottom lip, trying to picture the room finished with her things in it and not the way she remembered it from that night.

"Hey, where did you go there?" Kasper pulled her lip from her teeth with his thumb.

Blinking in surprise, she focused her eyes on him. "Just thinking."

"I'll be right here with you. I'll sleep on the floor next to the bed if that's what you need." He cupped her face with his big hands as he bent to stare into her eyes. "And if you don't want to stay here, you can stay with me. For as long as you want."

His lips were so close now. If she just leaned forward a little bit. The doorbell chimed loudly pulling a yelp from her.

"Pizza. Great, I'm starved." Kasper grinned before tearing down the steps to the front door.

The familiarity of hanging out alone with Kasper, eating pizza on a blanket, laughing like old times, was a balm to her soul. The way he laughed so open and honestly. Nothing fake about this version of Kasper. It was the version of Kass she thought of as hers all those years ago. The version he only showed her, period. She would let herself believe it again for a short time as long as he was here with her. She picked up their cups as Kasper grabbed the nearly empty pizza box. He slid the box into the fridge. His eyes went wide with shock as he turned to find her so close to him.

Without a word, Krysta took his hand in hers. She led him from the room up the stairs into her bedroom. The single bed they assembled while waiting for the pizza was the only furniture in the room. She stared into his eyes, never uttering a word. Instead she fingered the hem of his shirt before dragging it up and over his head.

Lust stormed in his eyes, burning as her fingers moved

to the button of his jeans. He grabbed her hand, stopping her.

"Kitten," he growled.

She knew exactly what that growl meant. Kasper cupped her cheek before sliding his hand to the nape of her neck slowly. He continued until his fingers tangled in her hair. He pulled, hard enough to make her spine tingle but not enough to hurt her. A breathy moan escaped her lips as his pressed into her jawline. He kissed her neck to her shoulders, across her collar bone before working his way up back to her lips. His kiss was punishing. His tongue dueled with hers. Wetness pooled in her panties. He tugged her hair again, positioning her face at the perfect angle to take the kiss even deeper.

She gripped his shoulders trying to hold on. Without any finesse, he relieved her of her shirt, tossing it across the room. Her bra was next. He unclasped and removed it like a magician. One minute it was there, the next her nipples were met with a cool breeze, making them pebble even harder. They ached for his touch, his mouth, his teeth. Fuck, she was practically a puddle of goo and they'd barely started.

Last night was good, but this, this was Kasper unleashed. The feral dominant animal he could become. She loved knowing she drove him crazy enough to bring it out of him. He unbuttoned her pants, dragging them and her panties down the legs she worked hard to keep toned. Instead of disposing of her panties like he had the rest of her clothes, he held them up, grinning. She felt exposed, standing there completely naked while he still had his pants on.

"On the bed, Kitten," he said, his voice gravelly with need.

She wasted no time crawling onto the mattress, her hands planted flat, her ass up in the air, presented like a gift. Instead of crawling up behind her, he walked around to the other side of the bed. The side she was facing.

"Come closer. This way."

She crawled on her hands and knees closer to the headboard.

"Good girl. Don't move."

He disappeared from her line of sight once more. The bed dipped behind her. She glanced over her shoulder. Fuck. He was magnificent. Her panties still clutched his hand, the intent in his eyes crystal clear.

"Hands," he ordered. Her body shuddered.

She redistributed her weight on her knees to balance. She held both hands up in the air. He looped her panties over one wrist, twisting the fabric to tighten its hold. Then he slipped the other wrist through the small open area left in the other leg hole. Gripping the middle of his makeshift restraints, Kasper leaned her forward, slipping the fabric over the knob on the headboard. She could feel his hard length pressed against her thigh. Twisting the fabric again, he doubled it over so she couldn't move her hands at all. The cloth bit into her wrists.

"Fucking beautiful."

He slapped her ass cheek, the sound crashing through the otherwise silent room. She moaned as another smack landed on the other cheek. The heat from his hand branded her skin. He glided his hand between her thighs, dragging it up to her center. With nothing more than a graze, he finally touched her where she wanted him to. No, needed him to. She needed him like air.

"Soaked. Just like I knew you'd be."

She couldn't speak. Every cell in her body was in a

holding pattern waiting for what this dominating man would do. Slowly, so fucking slowly, his finger penetrated her. He pumped it twice before adding another.

"You have no idea what you do to me."

She gasped as his cock replaced his fingers. Just the tip opened her up, stretching her lips.

"Tell me," she begged in a breathy voice.

"I'm not good with words when it comes to you." *That was a lie.* His words were everything. "How about I show you?"

He slammed the rest of the way into her in one long thrust. Krysta cried out, pleasure radiating through her. He alternated between rough slaps to her ass and caressing the globes with reverence. It didn't take long for the build up to hit its peak. He grabbed her chin, twisting her face to meet his eyes.

"Come. Fucking come all over my cock. I wanna feel this perfect pussy strangle my dick."

His eyes pierced hers as he delivered the dirty words she loved. She was right there on the precipice of detonation, unable to look away from him for even a moment. She couldn't even blink.

"I said come," he ordered.

That was it. She combusted. Her body sang with the most intense orgasm of her life. He smashed his lips to hers. Thrusting his tongue in sync with his cock, he consumed her cries. Once her body came down, he moved, gripping both hips with his hands. He pulled her body back further, sliding himself under her. Her body was suspended over the bed, wrists attached to the headboard still. When Kasper started moving inside her again, she felt like she was soaring.

His labored breaths and her moans bounced off the

bare walls, creating a surround sound effect. She would have bruises tomorrow. On her wrists, her hips. She didn't care in the slightest. It was an insignificant price to pay to have Kasper like this again. He had been a bossy lover before, but this was next level shit. She relished in it.

Kasper dipped his fingers between them for a moment. Before she realized what he was doing, his wet finger traced her puckered hole. He always told her he would take her there one day. He never got the chance before. He massaged her there with increased pressure with each stroke. She cried out, the sensation of his double penetration overwhelming. How could this feel so fucking good?

"Kasper," she cried out. "So good…yes…please…don't fucking stop."

"That's my girl. I can't hold it anymore. Come with me, Krysta."

And she did. Her eyes closed; starbursts of lights flashed behind her lids. Her walls pulsed around him. He yelled something unintelligible with one final thrust. Each pulse he emptied into her caused aftershocks, prolonging her own release. Slowly he pulled from her. She missed the contact immediately.

He wrapped one arm across her chest up between her breasts, then tugged at the binds on her wrists, tearing the material with the other hand. He lowered her gently to the mattress, scooching closer to her. Blood rushed to her hands as he rubbed each one between his own.

"Did I hurt you?" Concern laced his voice.

She placed a hand on his cheek. "No."

This kiss was gentle. She didn't know how long they shared the kiss that pierced her heart in a way she swore she wouldn't allow this time around.

"Let me clean you up."

He jumped up from the bed, stalking to the bathroom in all his naked glory. She laid there listening to him dig through a box for a moment, a smile on her face. He returned a few minutes later with a warm washcloth. He gently wiped away the evidence of their lovemaking. He leaned down, kissing each hip where he'd held on. Her heart galloped. Disposing of the washcloth, he climbed back into bed and tucked her under his arm, her head on his chest.

She wanted to tell him she still felt it. The undeniable connection they shared. She wanted to tell him she loved him, only she couldn't make the words come out. Instead, she placed a kiss above his heart and held him until she drifted off to sleep.

FOURTEEN
KASPER

THE WEEK WENT BY QUICKLY. The joy he got just being here with her each day was insurmountable. They had breakfast together each morning. He would leave for work after, she would finish up her work for the day when he got home. The evenings were spent talking while they ate take out. They made plans to go shopping for kitchen stuff this weekend. Then they would worship each other's bodies all evening until exhaustion made them collapse in each other's arms.

Wash. Rinse. Repeat.

He could do this every day for the rest of his life. With her. Only Krysta. He'd never had a connection like this with any other woman. He tried. He whored around for years, hoping for something to shake Krysta from his mind. No one came close. In fact, it was quite the opposite. Every meaningless bed he left in the middle of the night only added to the hole in his heart.

He needed to talk to Tank. Confess he was in love with Krysta. Beg him to accept it if that's what it came down to. He couldn't lose her again. This week showed him what a life together could look like. He wanted it. Wanted it so bad he could taste it.

Sunday morning Tank sent a group text inviting everyone over for dinner. Kasper could take this time to tell Tank his feelings—privately, of course. It would give him the added protection that if Tank tried to kill him, everyone would come to his aid. Well, maybe. Krysta wanted to finish up something she was working on, so she told him she'd be over in a few minutes. Everyone else had already arrived by the time he sauntered in.

"There you are." Tank clapped his back. "How's Krys doing? Nightmares?"

Kasper almost forgot the reason his best friend thought he was sleeping at his sister's place.

"She's been good. No nightmares that I'm aware of."

"That's great, man. I can't thank you enough."

"Actually—"

Kasper was interrupted by Mia's little squeals as she ran past them, leaping into Krysta's arms. She swung the little girl around before settling her on her hip. She listened to Mia babble on. Kasper rubbed the spot on his chest above his heart. Krysta looked like a natural with a toddler on her hip. What would she look like round with his baby growing inside that lush body?

Suddenly, he would give anything to know the answer to that question. Without a word, he left Tank standing there. He used the little girl as a cover, snatching her playfully from Krysta.

"We need to talk, Kitten."

She nodded quizzically. A strange odor wafted to his nose. He scrunched his nose, sniffing deeper to find the cause. Mia giggled in his arms.

"Good god, little darlin'. What did you do?"

Both ladies erupted with laughter.

"Max," he yelled. "What are you feeding this angel?"

Max grinned before plucking his daughter away from him. "Everything. She's like a bottomless pit. If Sloane is looking for me, tell her I'm changing Mia in the guest room."

Kasper pulled Krysta along behind him into the kitchen. She blushed when her eyes landed on the fridge. He loved that. He stole a quick kiss because how could he not.

"I want to tell him about us. Today. Now."

"What?" She took a step back. "Do you think we're at that point?"

"I think we're long past that point."

"I think we should wait a little longer."

Wait? Was she fucking joking? She practically begged for them to come clean with Tank for damn near three months before they split up six years ago. Now, he wanted to tell everyone as soon as possible. Especially his best friend and she didn't want to. He couldn't keep this from Tank anymore. His feelings for her aren't going to change. It's time they were honest from the beginning. Unless this was just fun for her.

"Are you ashamed to be with me? You wanna keep me your dirty little secret? Is that it?"

She shushed him. He was aware his voice had risen with each question he threw at her. He just didn't care.

"I'm not ashamed," she insisted.

"Then I'm telling him." He turned to go see Tank, but she grabbed his arm.

"We said we'd never tell him unless we were certain it was going somewhere."

"What the hell do you think was happening this last

week, Krys? Did you think I was going to walk away from you after what's been going on between us? After we fell asleep in each other's arms night after night?" He paced the length of the kitchen, rubbing his hands in his hair roughly. Heat flushed his body. His jaw started to ache from the way he clenched his teeth. "Or was I just a convenient fuck for you?"

"Kasper—"

"Hey guys." Sloane smiled as she disposed of a dirty diaper. "Is everything okay in here?" She eyed them suspiciously.

"I need some air." Krysta stormed out of the back door.

Kasper pounded his fist on the kitchen island and met Sloane's gaze. He was barely containing the hurt and rage battling within. She laid her hand on his shoulder. "I'll go talk to her. Everything will work itself out."

He nodded but couldn't bring himself to say anything.

FIFTEEN
KRYSTA

KRYSTA PRACTICALLY RAN out of Paxton's house. How could he ask her that? Of course, he wasn't just a fuck for her. He was everything. Every. Damn. Thing. If they confessed to Paxton, he would ask questions. If Kasper changed his mind again, it would damage his friendship with Paxton. She knew how important that relationship was to Kasper. She was giving him time to make sure this was what he truly wanted. Didn't he see that?

"Hey, you okay?" Sloane approached her, apprehension and worry etched on her face.

"Yeah, sorry."

You don't need to apologize, Krysta. I'm here for you if you need to talk. You know that, right?"

"I do. I don't know what I'm doing."

"Love will do that to you."

"I ended things with a perfectly nice, stable man."

"You did the right thing. He either didn't know the real you or wanted to change you into some prim and proper woman that we both know you would grow to resent sooner than later. Love isn't perfectly nice or stable. Love isn't perfect at all."

"I know you're right. I'm still scared."

She finally risked a glance at Sloane. She was taken completely off guard as two men came out of nowhere and grabbed Sloane. She flailed her arms and legs, trying to get free. She charged after them as they dragged her backward toward a white van with the side door standing open. Sloane's scream sliced through the quiet street like an explosion. Krysta never heard the other men come up behind her. A forearm closed around her throat as another encircled her arms, pinning them to her sides. She watched Sloane's body go limp. The men tossed Sloane in the van before heading her way.

She tried to scream and bite the hand covering her mouth. She couldn't make purchase on his skin. If she could make enough noise, she would alert the guys inside, if they weren't already. They would come running out and save them. She knew they would. Krysta tried screaming again. All her self-defense training kicked in. She tried stomping on her assailant's foot. Throwing an elbow into his gut, she wiggled, trying to break his hold. She flinched as she felt a pinch in the side of her neck. She felt her muscles relaxing even as she fought to retain control of her flailing limbs. The men carried her away, her view of the house fading into darkness.

SIXTEEN
KASPER

"EVERYTHING OKAY? WHERE'S KRYS?" Tank scowled when Kasper joined him in the living room.

"She's pissed at me. She walked outside to cool off. Sloane is with her."

Tank shook his head, chuckling. "What did you say to her now? If I didn't know any better, I'd think all your banter was foreplay."

He laughed like he said the joke of the century, only no one else joined him. The room was silent. A heaviness in the air. This was it.

"What's going on—"

Tank was stopped mid-sentence by a scream coming from outside. Tank, Foster, and Max bolted for the front door with Kasper right on their heels. He made it onto the porch as Max was bounding down the steps, his feet never seemed to touch the ground. Kasper caught an image of a woman lying in the open doorway of a white van before it slammed closed and sped off. Max continued to chase after it, while Tank was already on his cellphone. What the hell?

Kasper looked around. It was eerily quiet. That's when reality came crashing down on him.

"Who was in the van, Max?" He sprinted down the wooden stairs to meet Max in the yard. His heart pounded in his chest. "Where's Sloane? Krysta?"

Max was on his knees in the other neighbor's yard.

"Who was in the fucking van? Where are the girls?" Kasper enunciated each word. His stomach churned. Fire brewed under his skin.

"Truck." Max gasped for air.

"Which one?" Kasper was frantic. He could feel his blood boiling now. It really didn't matter which one. He loved them both in different ways. Either way it was go time, but he had to hear someone say it. It wouldn't be real until he said it.

"Both of them."

"Fuck!" Kasper roared.

"What's going on? You're scaring me." A very pregnant Marabella stood in the doorway with Cori. Both women had tears in their eyes. Marabella's eyes searched everywhere. Cori's eyes were burning a hole into Tank. They were searching for anything other than what really had just happened.

For a moment no one moved. Foster broke the heavy silence. "In the house, girls."

"But…" Marabella questioned, her arms cradling her swollen belly.

"No buts. Get in the damn house. Now. Everyone!" Foster bellowed. No one was stupid enough to argue with him. Except Kasper.

Kasper shook his head. "I can't just go sit inside and wait for someone to find their bodies. I need to find them now."

Tank grabbed his arm. "We'll find them. We just gotta think, Gutter."

Foster's smooth voice commanded the room. "This is what's going to happen. Max, Tank, get Mother on the line. Have him ping the girls' cellphones. If they still have them, it's a good place to start."

They both nodded and headed to the dining room where there was less noise. He was glad Foster took control. Max and Tank were too close to this one to think objectively. Shit, so was he. He wanted to smash things with his bare hands. He wanted to cause the kind of pain he was feeling, knowing it wouldn't take the pain away. Nothing would until the women were home safe.

"Cori, please take Bella and the kids upstairs. Take food and water up with you. Make sure the doors stay locked. If we need to bolt out of here, I don't want to leave you out in the open. Understood?"

"I know what to do, Foster," Marabella whispered.

Foster took her face in his hands. "Stay safe, I love you."

"Bring them home."

"We will," Foster promised his wife.

Cori ran to the kitchen to grab the things Foster told her to take upstairs. Marabella gathered the kids and up they went. She was a cop's wife. She knew what she needed to do if the shit hit the fan. She was well equipped to do it.

"Kasper."

Without hesitation, Kasper kicked into action. It had been a few years since he'd worn his blues, but just like that, he was ready to go into any situation with his brothers. "Whatever it is, consider it done."

"Benji."

That's all Foster had to say. Kasper left out the back door. He circled around the house, checking the perimeter before making a beeline to Krysta's place. He quickly unlocked the door, going straight to the laptop case he'd left lying on the kitchen counter. Snatching the bag, he tore out of there, jogging back to Tank's house.

Plopping his bag on the dining table, he pulled out his laptop and tapped the power button. While the machine hummed to life, he retrieved his gun from the small, zipped pouch on the case. He checked the weapon thoroughly. Once it was loaded, he secured it in his waistband at his back.

He sat down at the table. His fingers couldn't type fast enough as he sent an encrypted message to Benji. Benji was infiltrated deep. If he were going to find out for sure if the Petrov family was behind this, Benji would know. He hit send and waited. It only took about thirty seconds for him to get restless. He looked around the room. Tank and Max were on speaker phone with Mother. He was running a trace on Sloane's phone. Foster was on his phone, pacing back and forth. Kasper thought he'd said Brody. If that was the case, the officials were getting involved. That would muck up the water a bit, but they needed whatever help they could get to find the girls.

"Fuck!" he roared. Even he could hear the agony in his voice. "It's my fault. It's all my god damn fault."

Marabella gave him a sympathetic look as she scurried back down the stairs and into the kitchen. Foster zeroed in on her immediately.

"Bella?" he growled.

"Just forgot something. I'll only be a minute."

Tank crossed the room in three steps, taking Kasper's

shoulders in his hands. "Dude, you had nothing to do with this. Why the fuck would you even think that?"

"I pushed her too far. I pissed her off. If I'd just kept my mouth closed for once she wouldn't have been out there. Neither of them would." He tried to blink away the wetness he felt blurring his vision. This couldn't be happening.

He felt a hand on his shoulder. "You love her." Marabella's voice was eerily calm. Kasper turned. Her eyes brimmed with tears as she clutched a package of juice boxes to her chest. His selfish heart ached all over again for her. Sloane was her cousin. She was doing everything in her power to stay levelheaded. She was doing better than he was.

He nodded slowly. His eyes met Tank's. He was ready for whatever happened. Nothing could crush him more than he was at this very second. The woman he wanted to build a life with was out there somewhere held by dangerous men doing God only knew what to her and Sloane.

Tank continued to stare at him like an extinct bug.

"Go back upstairs. Keep those angels safe." Kasper kissed the top of her head. She was like a sister to him. His laptop dinged. Ignoring Tank, he rushed to it, ready to read Benji's short response.

Chatter here.
Girls in transit to unknown location.
In touch soon.

Petrov. Son of a bitch. He looked up to everyone staring at him, all anxious for an answer. Kasper nodded.

"Fuck! I'll tear that motherfucker apart with my bare

hands," Tank roared with enough pain and anger to do just that. Kasper hurried to where Tank slid down the wall. On his haunches, his head in his hands, Tank mumbled promises. To himself, the gods, Kasper didn't know. It didn't matter.

SEVENTEEN
KRYSTA

KRYSTA PEELED her dry eyes open. The artificial light in the room was too bright, causing her to squint until she adjusted. She rubbed her eyes, trying to focus them on her surroundings. She lay on a cot up against one side of the stark room. Everything was white and sterile, smelling of bleach and artificial lemons. It reminded her of a hospital room, only it wasn't. Sloane groaned from where she lay on an identical cot on the opposite end of the small room.

She stood up slowly, not yet trusting her legs. Once she was standing normally, she rushed to Sloane's side. "Sloane, are you okay?"

"Krysta?"

"Yeah."

Sloane pulled herself up into a seated position. "What the hell happened? One moment we were talking on the sidewalk and then everything started to swim." She brushed back the hair from her face.

"Someone grabbed us. That's all I know. I haven't seen or heard anyone. I can't figure out exactly where we are."

They both sat on Sloane's cot with their backs pressed

against the wall. Krysta looked at her watch. It was after three in the afternoon. Her watch. Her smart watch! She swiped on the small screen, excitement vibrating her bones. Only it was no help. There was no signal without her phone nearby. It was as useless as any analog watch.

Sloane scoffed. "No way it would have been that easy."

She shrugged. "A girl can dream." When she got out of this mess, she was investing in a newer model that ran on cellular data.

"That she can."

"How long do you think we've been missing?"

"A couple hours I'd guess."

"I'm scared," Sloane admitted as she grabbed Krysta's hand.

She squeezed it gently in return. "I know, me too."

Voices drew both of their attention to the door. They stilled, trying to garner any information they could. Krysta couldn't make out what they were saying. They were muffled and didn't sound right. Maybe the drugs they used on her were affecting her still.

"Russian," Sloane whispered.

Things went from bad to worse. They were fucked. The Russians didn't play around, that Krysta was certain of. The guys had to know they were missing by now. She knew they'd do everything they could to find them, but she also knew that it wasn't a guarantee they'd be found in time. Or found at all if that was what these guys intended. Millions of women and girls went missing every year in the US to sex trafficking rings.

Therefore, she had to figure out an escape. The door opened, a short weasel-looking man strolled in. He wore a black suit. Krysta had no idea what designer brand it was, though she had no doubts it was expensive. His dark brown beady rat eyes were too small for his face, while his black hair came to rest on the tops of his shoulders. He stood in the middle of the room, his gaze raking over them. When he spoke, his English was heavily accented.

"Two for the price of one." He chuckled smugly.

Neither of the women replied. The man clasped his hands behind his back. He continued as he began pacing, not in a nervous way. It was like a businessman addressing a boardroom of colleagues beneath his status.

"Mrs. Fear, you've done well evading my associates. That is all over now. My father believed you were no threat to us. He grew soft in his old age. I am not."

Sloane didn't bother correcting him. She wasn't Mrs. Fear yet, not that it would make a difference to these dick nuggets.

"So why haven't you just killed us yet?" Krysta asked bluntly.

"Why waste a good product?" The weasel smiled. "A good businessman could make a lot of money with girls looking like you. I'm nothing if not a good businessman."

"You sound like a sleazeball," she spat at him.

Without another word, he strolled out of the room, his guards following behind him. Sloane squeezed her hand again. Krysta knew their time being held here was growing shorter each moment. They couldn't be moved to a second location. It was the worst possible scenario. It would be harder for the guys to find them. Unfortunately, she had no idea what to do. At least not yet.

A couple hours passed before Sloane broke the silence. "So, what really happened?"

"With what?"

"Kasper. I know there's more than whatever happened today."

"Is this really the place to have this conversation?" Krysta wrinkled her nose.

"Who knows how long we'll be stuck here? Think of it as confession, you know...in case." She shrugged. "Plus, a distraction could do us both some good right now."

Krysta looked down at her hands. Picking at her nails, she thought about her past and all she kept hidden from everyone all these years. Maybe it would be good to get it off her chest with someone she trusted. She could get a different perspective from someone who wasn't invested.

"He abandoned me when I needed him the most." Tears filled her eyes as she pressed on.

"We had been seeing each other in secret. Paxton would've been pissed and neither of us wanted their friendship in danger if we decided it wasn't right. Kasper didn't have it easy growing up. He spent more of his time with us than with his own family. We just wanted to be sure, ya know?"

"That sounds reasonable."

Krysta nodded in agreement. "After six of the most amazing months of my life, I wanted to come clean with Paxton. That's not entirely true. I wanted to tell him a few weeks into the relationship. Other than all the sneaking around, our relationship was everything I'd been hoping for. Kasper eventually agreed but asked that we wait a few weeks until they were done with the academy. Of course, I agreed. I knew they were under a lot of stress preparing for exams."

Krysta stood up, pacing the small room. Her hands shook from the onslaught of hurt rushing back in. A tear slipped free; she could feel the warm liquid slowly drag down her cheek. "I found out I was pregnant two weeks later. He closed off completely. He told me he wasn't ready for that kind of responsibility. Like I was—I was almost nineteen and the only family I had left was Paxton. I was scared and then I was alone."

"Oh, Krysta. I know how that feels. I ran from Max and kept my pregnancy a secret. I know how scary that is. I couldn't imagine going through that at nineteen."

"I went to my twelve weeks checkup and the doctor was acting strange. He had multiple technicians come in with different machines until finally he confessed, he was unable to find a heartbeat. I thought that would be the worst day of my life until he told me the baby was too far along to risk using medicine to clear out my uterus. I needed a D&C and had to wait three days for an open spot in the operating room."

Sloane hurried to her feet and threw her arms around Krysta. Krysta squeezed her back, both openly crying. Both momentarily forgetting they were locked in a room while their lives were in danger. At that moment, Krysta was back to being a nineteen-year-old woman, scared and alone.

The doctors told her she couldn't drive herself. The anesthesia would still be in her system. Kasper hadn't returned any of her calls or texts since she told him she was keeping the baby the month before. What was she going to tell Paxton? Certainly not the truth. She checked her face in the rearview mirror. Her eyes were red and puffy. She ran her fingers through her hair before getting out of her car.

Paxton opened the front door, blocking the entrance with his massive frame.

"Where ya been?" The smile fell from his lips. "What happened? What's wrong?"

"I'm okay, let's go inside and I'll tell you."

She sat next to him on the worn couch. "I'm going to be fine. I need a ride on Thursday to the hospital. I wasn't feeling well so I went to see my gynecologist, they found a polyp in my uterus that needs removing." She'd rehearsed the lie after doing some research online.

"Are you sure it's safe? Why didn't you tell me you weren't feeling well? I knew something was off with you."

He pulled her into his comforting embrace. It took all the strength she possessed to not break down like she had the whole drive home. She had to pull over two different times before she caused an accident. She hated lying to him about this, but there was no other way. It would ruin the friendship he had with Kasper. They were brothers in every way but blood. She knew better than to get involved with Kasper.

"You can count on me. I'll be there, anything you need. Love you, little sis."

"I love you too."

Sloane's voice brought her back to the present. "I can't imagine what that must've been like for you."

"It was the worst day of my life, and I went through it alone. I begged his voicemail multiple times asking him to call me back that day and he never did. Instead, he came by the house after I was home to pick up Paxton. They were going on a double date. I don't know if I can truly get past that. I loved him so much, I almost forgot what I deserved." Krysta swiped away the tears, drying her hands on her denim-clad thighs.

She continued, "I still love him, if I'm being honest. He's been staying with me since the Friday after Thanksgiving."

"Staying with you or *staying with you*?" Sloane waggled her eyebrows.

"We've been sleeping together. Everything has been amazing, I'll be the first to admit that. I'm fucking scared, though. You see what he's like. He's still a playboy. I can't and won't compete with the revolving door of women he has."

"Has he been seeing or talking to anyone while he's staying there?"

"No. That I do know. That doesn't guarantee he won't. I don't know if I can risk that. Sometimes love just isn't enough."

Sloane smiled softly. "But...sometimes love conquers all."

EIGHTEEN
KASPER

IT HAD BEEN hours since the girls had been abducted from the front lawn. He was losing his mind thinking of all the things that could be happening to Krysta. Was she hurt? Scared? Did she know he wouldn't stop looking for her? He wanted to kill every man who dared put a hand on her. How could he let this happen? They let their guard down, that's how. One minute they're laughing then fighting and now... now he was dying inside. He could still smell the roasted chicken in the air. The table was set for a family dinner that wouldn't be eaten tonight.

Foster and Max went upstairs to check on Marabella and the kids. Hopefully Cori has helped her keep the kids calm. Tank was back to studying him from his place on the floor. "We need to talk. Now."

Fuck. That was never a good sign. He nodded, holding out a hand for Tank. He took it and Kasper helped him to his feet. Tank walked through the kitchen and out the back door. Once he was in the middle of the yard, he turned around, crossing his arms over his chest.

"Talk." He glared.

"I'm in love with your sister."

"How long?"

"A long fucking time." Kasper linked his fingers behind his head, his eyes rolled skyward.

"How long?" he spit out. Kasper met his gaze.

"I knew I wanted her when she was a senior in high school. I never touched her though. I swear on my life." Kasper inhaled deeply before continuing. "Not until her eighteenth birthday when I kissed her."

"Was it you? Were you the father? Don't even try to lie to me, not after everything we've been through. I don't know why I didn't see it before. I must've been fucking blind."

Kasper ran his hands over his face. He didn't want to have this conversation now. He wanted to focus all his attention on finding their women. He couldn't remain silent. It was time to fess up to everything.

"Yeah, it was, but I fucked up. I panicked. I never meant to hurt her. You gotta believe me," he pleaded.

"You knocked up my baby sister and dumped her. That's what you're telling me?" Tank's face was growing redder by the second. His fists clenched by his sides. Kasper had never been the object of Tank's rage. He hadn't seen this side of him in a while. He deserved it, though.

"I'm sorry—"

His words were stopped short when Tank's fist snapped his head back. Pain blossomed across his jaw. He licked the blood from his lips.

"Let me explain, please?" He knew Tank pulled his punch. If he'd really punched him, Kasper would be down for the count.

"I'm listening. I can't promise I won't finish breaking your face when you're done, though. Best friend or not."

"Fair enough. On Krysta's eighteenth birthday, I kissed her. I had wanted to for months, but I kept my distance. She was all dressed up, about to go on a date with some asshole and I couldn't let someone like that be the first guy to kiss that amazing woman. I thought I'd get her out of my system. What's one kiss? I know how that sounds, man. I really do, but I'm being honest with you here."

"Continue," Tank growled. His fists turned white by his side again.

"I fell. Hard. Being with her was beyond my wildest dreams. We'd been seeing each other for over six months. We were going to go public after we graduated the academy. Then she told me she was pregnant, and I panicked. I needed time to think. I was terrified. You know what my dad was like. The only role model I had was your dad. I couldn't stop thinking about how disappointed he would have been. Then a few weeks later, she texts me. She said she didn't want to raise a child without a father, and I was a piece of shit. She was right. She was absofuckinlutely right." More tears welled in his eyes.

Tank scrubbed his hands over his bald head. "The only thing my father, and myself—for the record—would have been disappointed in, was the fact you kept it a secret and you abandoned her when she needed you. My sister was a wreck when she lost that baby."

Wait, what? Kasper had to have heard him wrong. That couldn't be right. "She told you that? She lost the baby? I always thought she…" He trailed off, unable to voice what he thought.

"I was in the recovery room with her, she was still out of it. At first, I thought she was talking nonsense. She said her baby died. The way she sobbed…" Tank hung his head, momentarily lost in a memory. "…it was haunting.

Curiosity got the best of me. I read her chart on the table. She never remembered telling me because of the anesthesia and I never brought it up. That's not something she needed to relive."

"I had no idea. No matter what I did back then, I loved her. I still love her, with everything I am. I promise you, I'm gonna make things right."

"I love you like a brother, but I can't see my sister get hurt again. No more lies. No more games. If you can't be in it one hundred percent, then let her go."

"I swear to you, Tank. That's why we argued earlier. I wanted to tell you about us today. She didn't. I'm all in this time," Kasper promised his best friend as he walked away from him.

"We have to find her first," Tank called over his shoulder as he marched back into the house. Kasper launched a nearby folding chair across the yard. With a deep breath, he went back into the house. The house was as silent as a tomb. He sat in front of his laptop, willing it to chime with a response from Benji.

Benji was still with the Bush Castle PD. He'd been in deep cover for three years. He'd infiltrated the Petrov family as a low-level gun for hire, working his way up in the ranks quickly. Taking down one arm of the Russian mob had been all consuming for him. Kasper had only seen him a few times in the past year—the most recent was little Mia's birthday party. He'd looked haunted when they found him in Max's living room. He tried to hide it, but Kasper knew that look in his eyes. Their conversation had been enlightening.

"Man, it's so good to see you." Benji grabbed Kasper in a one-armed hug.

"We weren't sure if you'd be able to make it. It's good to see you too."

Kasper looked Benji over. He had put on a lot of muscle, but there were dark circles under his eyes.

"You doin' okay, man?"

Benji scrubbed his fingers though his long black hair. "I know what I'm doing is for the greater good, but sometimes it takes a toll. I'm tired. Physically yes, but also mentally."

Kasper had never been a part of a long-term operation. He could only imagine the weight of his situation. Lying to everyone you meet and pretending you're someone you're not. He was never great at deception. Usually, he was brutally honest.

"It's rough, I'm sure." Kasper clapped his back, feeling the hollowness in his words.

"There's this girl…" Benji smiled.

"Now we're talking," Kasper cocked a brow in surprise, rubbing his hands together enthusiastically. "Tell me about her."

"She's everything I've ever wanted, and even though I know it'll never work out; I can't seem to stay away from her. She's beautiful, for sure, but so much more. Her dark sense of humor contrasts with her sunny personality. Smart, damn, is she the smartest woman I've ever met. Being with her is like a drug I can't get enough of."

"It sounds like you're head over heels. Things will work out. Just give it time. This case will hopefully be over soon and you two can take a much-needed vacation."

Benji shook his head in rebuttal. "No, it won't. She's Sophia Petrov."

Kasper whistled, "Damn…that's…"

"I know," Benji took a deep breath. "Let's talk about some-

thing a little lighter. Tank know you're in love with his sister yet?"

Had everyone known besides Tank? Kasper startled when his computer dinged. Everyone turned to watch him in anticipation of whatever Benji had to say. He quickly typed in his password as he held his breath, waiting for the worst news.

Girls alive.
Multiple locations possible:
Warehouse district on the north end
Safe house on Cherry Hill Lane
Bush Castle Asylum

Kasper waited for more for information, but none came. They had three possible locations for the girls. Tank paced the room. It was Max who spoke up first.

"We should split up. Foster and I will go to the warehouses. Tank and Gutter can go check out the safe house."

Tank stood still finally. "You wanna send two guys into a mob situation with two hostages? What about the asylum? Who's gonna check there?"

"You have a better suggestion? As for the Asylum, whoever clears their location first goes there," Foster chimed in.

Kasper nodded in agreement. "I think we'd cover more ground that way."

"What about Mother?" Kasper asked as he packed up his laptop, zippered the carrier, and slung it over his shoulder. He was ready to go.

"He's checking out traffic cam footage and coordinating with Brody. Once we know their location, he'll send a team."

"Let's get the hell outta here then." Without waiting, Kasper hurried out the front door, waiting by Tank's car for him to move his ass. His bike would be faster, but he'd left that at his apartment. Plus, it was a hell of a lot louder. The element of surprise was key.

NINETEEN
KRYSTA

KRYSTA DIDN'T KNOW how long they had been here. She was hungry and thirsty. She knew Sloane had to be too. They had to make it out of this place. She couldn't leave Paxton. She was the only blood family he had left. Sloane and Max were getting married in a few months. This was not where their story ended.

One thing was for sure, a situation like this really opened her eyes. If she got out of this, no—when she got out of this, she would tell Kasper her feelings. Life was too short not do everything in her power to be as happy as she could be. She was madly in love with him.

Sloane sobbed next to her, her knees pulled up to her chest, her arms wrapped around them tightly. Krysta didn't have many encouraging words to say. Instead, she decided to distract her.

"Before you know it, the guys will find us. Then you and Max can practice for your honeymoon." She smiled.

She lifted her head. "You really think they're going to find us?"

Krysta wasn't going to lie to her friend by telling her

everything was going to be all right. She honestly didn't know if they would find them in time, but she did know they would never give up. That was the best comfort she could give.

"I know they'll never stop looking. If they won't give up on us, we won't give up on them."

Sloane nodded sadly in agreement.

"I know it's a horrible thing to say, but I'm glad you're stuck here with me. I can't imagine being in this place all by myself." She wrapped her arms around Krysta.

They leaned against each other. Krysta's thoughts bounced back and forth between praying the men found them and hoping she could get them free. Eventually the silence and the lack of things to keep her occupied caused her eyes to get heavy. She slowly drifted off to sleep.

Startled awake at the sound of the door opening, Sloane grabbed ahold of her hand.

"Rise and shine, ladies." Dick-face number one smiled with all the friendliness of a crocodile. "Boss wants you moved. He's got a buyer lined up for you, doll face." He winked at Sloane.

"We're not going anywhere with you." Krysta was proud of herself for keeping, mostly, calm. Her brain kept screaming *no, no, no.* She knew the odds of being found if they moved them. They'd be another statistic. She knew she had to stall if she had any hope left to come up with a plan to get away.

"You don't have a fucking choice," Number two sneered, stepping closer.

Krysta clenched her fist. When he reached for her, she lashed out letting her rage fuel her movements. Her fist hit its target. Dick-face number two howled in pain, grabbing his nose. Blood started to seep between his fingers.

Number one started yelling in Russian. She had no idea what he was saying. He sounded pissed. He smacked her across the face hard enough to give her whiplash. The coppery taste of blood coated her tongue.

"You hit like a bitch," she sneered with as much bravado as she could muster. Her pulse throbbing through her head.

She refused to let them see her fear. They were like sharks when they smelled blood in the water. She wasn't chumming it for them.

Sloan was screaming and crying from her place on the dirty mattress. Yelling like a banshee to distract them from Sloane, Krysta threw herself at him. Swinging her fists wildly, she landed a few punches to his face. He back-handed her this time, the force knocking her to the concrete floor. Grabbing her hair roughly, he pulled her head up to face him. She was twisted in an awkward angle, the concrete digging into her knees. An evil grin spread across the face of the madman holding her.

"Maybe you and I will have a little fun before we leave." He grabbed ahold of his crotch, eyes gleaming in anticipation. "Maybe then you'll learn to keep your mouth shut."

"I'll bite off anything you put in there." She spat blood onto his shoes.

He pulled on her hair harder, a whimper escaped her lips. He raised his right arm about to land another blow to her face.

"Bitch, I'll—"

Gunfire rang out from somewhere on the property. Her lips curved into a sinister grin up at the man holding her hostage. His face was red, twisted in rage.

"That's right, motherfucker, you're a dead man." She sing songed.

His arm was still raised in his attempt to subdue her. Dick number two's head shot around to his partner. He was breathing heavily through his mouth. "What the fuck was that?"

Without answering, her captor grabbed her upper arm while keeping his left hand in her hair, pulling her to her feet.

"We need to get them out of here. Get the other one."

Using their bodies as human shields, the men opened the door and stepped out into an empty hallway. The gray paint was peeling off the walls. Leaves and debris were scattered over the linoleum. It was a stark difference between the sterile room they had been in. As if she weren't scared enough, it only added to the fear rattling around her brain. They were being dragged down the long hallway. The elevator ahead dinged the arrival of the car stopping on their floor. She whipped her head toward the sound.

Her heart leapt in her throat as she recognized, even from this distance, her brother step from the elevator car. She'd never seen this side of him. If she didn't know him, she would have been terrified. The rage on his face was palpable. Kasper was a mirror image, coming out of the elevator right behind him. Krysta screamed, tears freely rolling down her cheeks. She fought to break free from her jailer even as he pulled her by her hair. Kasper's head swiveled in her direction, his hard stare blazing with murderous intent. As scared as she was, she still couldn't help herself from going gooey inside. Kasper was hot as fuck when he was unleashed.

Screaming in Russian, the men holding them retreated

the way they came. They yanked them through the door to the stairwell at the opposite end of the hallway. Sloane tripped a few times. Krysta didn't know if she was doing it on purpose to slow them down or if she was so distraught, she couldn't walk straight.

Krysta was grateful Sloane was slowing them down, regardless. At least she was grateful, until the dickhead whose nose she broke smashed the butt of his gun into Sloane's face. She screamed in agony.

"Get moving," he ordered, continuing down the steps.

"Fuck you," she barked back vehemently.

Krysta would have laughed in any other situation. Sloane didn't usually drop the F bomb. Krysta was the mouthy one out of all the women. She heard heavy boots stomping up the stairs from below them moments before she the door smashed open above them. She had no idea how many men were coming up the stairs. She prayed Paxton and Kasper would be able to handle them.

———

KASPER

They burst through the heavy wood door and into the stairwell. She was still alive. That was enough for now. It had to be. He would worry about everything else after they were safe. Kasper could make out voices below them. Peeking over the side, he scanned the stairwell. They were close. He could see the girls. Taking two steps at a time, they were only three floors above where Sloane and Krysta were, and they were closing the distance at a remarkable speed. Their captors continued dragging them down each step as fast as they could without removing the guns pressed to their heads until they stopped short.

"Let them go!" Kasper heard Max yell from somewhere below them. Thank God.

Slowing down their descent, Kasper and Tank drew their side arms up. He could see the girls on a landing between two floors. With guns drawn, they approached from above. One of the captors turned to face them as the other continued to stand off with Max and Foster. He was tall with short black hair. His nose was bent funny, as if it had been broken one too many times.

Krysta stood stock still. The man had one arm around her shoulders, using her as a human shield, the other held a gun to her head. Her face was showing the signs of impending bruises. Blood was evident around her mouth and above her left eye. He seethed inside.

"Don't come any closer," the man warned, like he was controlling this situation. He wasn't calling the shots. His minutes were numbered.

"We will kill them both," his partner cried out. His Russian accent was even thicker than the man holding Krysta.

"Are you all right?" Max called up to his future wife. Kasper refused to think of her any other way. They would get them out of here and Max would marry her as soon as he could.

"I am now," she whispered.

Kasper couldn't take his eyes off Krysta, still cataloging what injuries he could see. He noticed in addition to the beginning of the black eye forming, her lip was actually split, and he could see the knot on her forehead above the bloody brow from where he stood.

"Krys." It was the only word Tank said.

"Don't worry about me. I'm fine. He hits like a bitch." Her grin was wicked.

"Let us by or I'll put a bullet in her brain." The Russian's hand was shaking slightly.

Tank and Kasper didn't lower their weapons. Kasper wouldn't look away from Krysta to see what Max and Foster were doing. He'd hoped they were holding their positions.

Krysta growled through clenched teeth. "Stop thinking, guys. You know what happens with women sold into human trafficking. I'd be better off dead. So, kill this ugly motherfucker now."

Krysta brought her elbow back, slamming into the bastard's solar plexus. Pride swelled in him. That was his girl. Everything seemed to move in slow motion from that point. The assailant's gun lowered slightly as he huffed out a breath from the impact. Kasper didn't waste a second. He pulled the trigger twice. The man's body shook multiple times. That's when Kasper realized Tank had fired at the same time. Everything resumed its normal speed the moment Kasper's gaze found Krysta's.

He could hear other shots echo in the stairwell. He trusted Max and Foster to handle shit. He rushed to Krysta, who was on her knees now with her hands covering her head. Tank was right beside him, pulling Krysta into his arms. Kasper glanced over to find Max holding Sloane. Both the Russians were dead, multiple shots to the head. He wanted to rush to her, to be the one to comfort Krysta. His fingers itched to touch her as she clung to her brother.

"Guys, we gotta get outta here. This place is crawling with more of these assholes. Let's move," Foster ordered. They all started down the steps moving quickly. Max and

Foster took the lead. Krysta and Sloane walked side by side in front of Tank and Kasper. He didn't miss the way Krysta favored her right leg.

"Which one of you has an extra piece?" Krysta asked over her shoulder.

Without a word, Tank stopped. Pulling his spare from his ankle holster, he handed it over butt first. She accepted it with a wicked sneer before checking the magazine and chamber.

"Thanks, big brother. It's good to see you guys, but what took you so long? Did ass-face need to fix his hair?" she joked, nodding to Kasper.

That's what she did. Kasper knew she used humor to help keep her calm. They needed all the calm they could get. Plus, she was sexy as hell fired up. He was more than happy to spar with her.

"I had to finish cooking dinner, since you two decided it was break time."

"I hope you basted it. I don't like dry chicken."

"You don't have to worry your pretty little head, I always make sure things are nice and juicy, Kitten."

"I'm not eating that chicken anymore," Max called from the exit door.

They all chuckled dryly as they gathered alongside Max. The tension was high. His heart raced as his chest tightened. They weren't in the clear yet. They had no idea what or who would be waiting on the other side of the door. There could be twenty mob guys ready to shoot first and take hostages second. They needed to get the girls to safety. They'd worry about Petrov later if need be.

"When we get out of here, move quickly and quietly. There are two vehicles. Krysta, you go with Tank and

Gutter. Sloane is with Max and me," Foster directed everyone.

Kasper touched her arm gently. "Kitten, are you good?"

She glared at him for a moment. Her eyes softened slightly. "Nothing I can't handle."

He nodded to Max. Wrapping his arm around Sloane to help steady her, Max opened the door. One by one they ran toward the vehicles they'd stashed by the road just before the entrance to the asylum. It was about a quarter of a mile ahead. Krysta's limp was getting worse with each step. She cried out, falling to her knees. Kasper hurried back to her.

"Get up, Kitten."

Helping her stand, he kept ahold of one arm as he bent over, putting his shoulder into her belly and lifted. Situated into a fireman's carry, Kasper picked up the pace.

"Kass, what are you doing?" she screeched. "This is slowing you down."

"Watch my six, Kitten. I'm getting you outta here."

She used his belt as leverage to push herself up so she could lift her head. The SUVs were in sight. Kasper picked up his speed to an all-out sprint.

"Two coming up behind us," she called. "I can't get a clear shot like this."

They made it to the vehicles just as shots rang out. Foster already had the door open and was crouched behind it, returning fire. Rushing behind Tank's truck, Kasper gently placed Krysta on her feet. Max pushed Sloane into the backseat of the SUV. He slammed the door shut behind her before jumping into the driver's seat. Tank was returning fire from across the hood of his truck.

Kasper turned to grab a hold of Krysta once more, only she wasn't there. What the fuck?

Turning around again, his blood ran cold. Petrov stood not twenty feet behind their position. Fresh tears streamed down Krysta's battered face with yet another gun pressed to her temple. He was frozen in place.

"Tank," was all he could say through clenched teeth.

He didn't see Tank's expression when he assessed the situation, he was too focused on her. Her hands gripped Petrov's arm that circled her slender throat. Her chin quivered, but her gaze was glued to him.

Two men sauntered up behind Petrov, guns trained on him and Tank. Surprise broke his stupor. Benji winked at him. That sneaky bastard. Kasper could kiss him.

"This one is going to be my new pet, boys." Petrov glided the gun barrel down the length of Krysta's jaw.

Without any preamble, Benji swung his arm toward the man standing smugly beside him. Another one of Petrov's top men, no doubt. He squeezed the trigger. Blood sprayed from the man's head. He dropped like a puppet whose strings were cut. Petrov's eyes bugged from his head. He took the gun off Krysta, firing twice at Benji.

"Down, Krys!" Tank ordered. She spun out Petrov's grasp, dropping to one knee.

Tank fired, silencing everything except Kasper's heart thundering in his chest. Krysta ran for him like the devil himself was chasing her. In a way, he had. Leaping into his arms, she wrapped her legs around his waist, burying her face into his shoulder. She sobbed, squeezing him tighter.

"I got you," he whispered in her ear.

"Benji's been hit," Tank yelled.

He ran for Tank, his girl still in his arms. She jumped down to crouch beside their friend.

"You crazy son of a bitch." Krysta pushed the hair back from Benji's face.

It twisted in agony as Tank tore his t-shirt open to assess the damage. Kasper noted two bullet holes. One in the shoulder and another in the belly. He was bleeding bad.

"We gotta get him to a hospital."

"I know. Krys, grab my first aid kit from behind the seat and any rags or blankets. I think I have one or two in there."

She disappeared from his side, returning a few minutes later. Kasper took the kit from her. Opening the lid, he rifled through the contents. There was one package of Hemostat powder. It wouldn't be enough for both entry points, but it could help slow the bleeding enough. Kasper ripped the package open, pouring the powder on Benji's stomach wound. Krysta was applying pressure to his shoulder as Tank ripped a shirt into rags.

Quickly they worked to patch him up enough to give him a fighting chance.

TWENTY
KRYSTA

PAXTON WHIPPED the truck into the emergency room bay. Krysta almost toppled on top of Benji from the sudden stop. Paxton quickly got out of the truck, looking into the bed where she and Kasper continued to apply pressure to Benji's injuries. There was so much blood. She prayed the entire ride here for a miracle. Paxton sprinted through the emergency room doors. Krysta recognized his voice booming over the crowd, but she couldn't make out what he was saying. He returned in seconds with a gurney manned by nurses hot on his heels.

She climbed out of the truck, giving the hospital staff room to work. Benji grunted in pain as the male nurses began strapping him to the back board before moving him onto the gurney. They were talking over his body in lingo she couldn't decipher. Once they had him on the gurney, he spoke for the first time since they put him in the truck.

"Krys?"

"Yeah, Ben?"

"What the hell happened to your face?" His top lip

curled just a bit. A tease of a grin. Fuck, she hoped that wasn't the last time she saw it. These guys lived to tease each other, so this had to be a good sign.

She felt the smile spread across her face, pulling at the cut on her lip. She winced. Her fingertips automatically reached up to touch it. "I got bored while I waited for you guys, so I punched myself a few times." She winked playfully. "What the fuck took you so long?"

Benji was whisked away before he could respond. Kasper chuckled, earning him a sly smile from her. He was smeared with blood. They all were. Blood coated her trembling hands. Some of it had already dried, but she smeared what she could off on her shirt. It was ruined already anyway. Without preamble, she marched to Kasper's side. Slipping her arms around his waist, she tucked herself under his arm. It didn't matter if Paxton was watching her like a hawk while he talked on his phone. She needed to be held by him. She needed to feel the rhythm of his heart under her cheek.

Kasper pushed her hair from her face, tipping her head up. "We need to get you checked out."

"I'm fine."

"You aren't."

"I am. A few bruises, that's all."

"You aren't, you stubborn ass woman. Your head is bleeding, and you need an x-ray on that leg you're limping on."

"Can't I just hold you?"

His eyes softened. "Every fucking day, Kitten. However, right now we need to get you checked out." He swept her up in his arms. She put her head back on his shoulder.

"Go on in," Paxton called over. "I'll wait for everyone else. Max is bringing Sloane. She took a bad hit in the face. Coincidentally, Bella's stress seems to have sent her into labor, so they stopped to get her first."

"Oh my god," she gasped.

"I'll be with her, let us know when they get here or if there are any updates on Benji."

———

A few hours had passed since they'd arrived at Bush Castle Memorial Hospital. Krysta felt the fatigue in every cell in her body. She sat on a couch in the surgical waiting room with Paxton, Cori, and Kasper. Her head rested on Kasper's chest as he rubbed aimlessly up and down her arm.

Benji was still in the operating room. Marabella was up three floors in labor and delivery, where Max and Sloane waited for Foster to update them. Her water broke, but she was still only eight centimeters dilated the last time they heard from him. That was about fifteen minutes ago. Sloane was lucky her face wasn't fractured. She had a concussion and plenty of ugly bruises on her face and arms. She would be just fine. Krysta had twisted her ankle, but it wasn't anything serious. She'd be sore for a while.

A woman in blue scrubs came out of the operating room. She pulled her mask down, scanning the waiting room. "Family of Benjamin Agani?"

"That's us," Paxton answered as they all stood in unison.

"Mr. Agani is stable. The less severe shoulder wound was a through and through. We patched that one without incident. The one to the abdomen was trickier. How the bullet didn't hit any major organs is a mystery. The bullet was a tenth of an inch from hitting his spine between the L1 and L2 vertebrae. We've given him a transfusion of blood."

Cori spoke up first. "He's going to be okay?"

"We won't know for another twenty-four hours, but I'm optimistic."

They thanked the doctor, resuming their seats. It was going to be a long night. She was starving and yet, so exhausted, she didn't think she could eat even if she tried.

"So this is a thing now?" Tank nodded toward them.

Kasper's fingers stilled on her skin. She felt his muscles tense under her. Wrapping her arm around his chest, she met Paxton's gaze. "Would you have a problem if it was?"

"Would it matter if I did?" His expression never wavered. Cori, however, grinned like the cat that ate the canary.

Slowly she shook her head. "Not in the least. Not to me, anyway."

Kasper sucked in a breath. As he released it, his body relaxed under her once more. A smirk spread across her brother's face.

"Gutter," he said to Kasper.

Lifting her head, she let her gaze swivel between the two most important men in her life. Kasper raised his head, looking to his best friend without saying anything. The apprehension of what Paxton would say shone through his eyes and the set of his jaw.

"Don't fuck it up, brother." He chortled.

Krysta's heart overflowed with love. She couldn't imagine being happier than she was right now knowing Paxton was good with her relationship with Kasper. When she really thought about it, she wondered why she was worried in the first place. Sure, when she was eighteen, he would have had issues, but she was a grown woman now. She knew without a doubt he only wanted her to be happy.

Kasper practically beamed. Cuddling her closer, he kissed her forehead. "I don't intend to."

TWENTY-ONE
KASPER

"BENJI NEEDS someone to break him out of the hospital. I'm going with Tank to bust him out," he said as he leaned down to kiss Krysta's bare shoulder where she still lay in bed.

Her legs were spread wide under the sheet, taking up as much real estate as possible while her hands stayed tucked close under her pillow. The sheet rested just above her tantalizing ass. He wanted to slither back into bed and ravish her again, but he had things to do.

"Don't get in any trouble. I'm too worn out to have to come post bail." She grinned, never opening her eyes.

"Eyes," he demanded.

Instantly they opened, pupils dilating. Fuck, she was perfect. The way she looked at him, with lust, adoration, and so much fucking love. He never imagined someone could love him the way she did. Mind, body, and soul. She was a balm to his soul. She was everything. That's why after they sprung Benji, he was going with Tank to find something that sparkled as much as she did.

———

They sauntered into Benji's room. Tank stopped abruptly, causing Kasper to slam into his back. "What the fuck, dude?"

Tank stepped to the side to make room for him to enter the room. A woman sat next to Benji's bedside holding his hand. She stood quickly when they entered. She was attractive. Her long blonde hair hung straight as a pin. Her body though, was all curves. She chewed her bottom lip.

"Guys, this is Sophia." Benji sat up in bed. He winced as he swung his legs over the side. "Hand me those clothes, will ya, Doll?"

"Hey," Tank and Kasper said in unison.

"Hi," she addressed them as she handed Benji his belongings. "I better go."

She hesitated for a moment, then leaned over, kissing Benji's cheek. She whispered something in his ear, earning her a smirk. She hurried out of the room.

"Sophia?" Kasper questioned. "As in *the* Sophia?"

He nodded, buttoning his pants, the waistline just below the white bandage covering one of the bullet holes. A matching one adorned his shoulder.

"I feel like I missed something." Tank rubbed his bald head.

"That's no surprise. You miss a lot of shit." Benji laughed.

"Even you knew about dipshit and my sister, didn't you?"

"I'm a detective, remember? You must suck as an investigator. Why does Maxie Pad keep you around?" He snickered.

"Fuck you. Walk home."

"I take it back. Get me the fuck outta here."

"Okay, but I wanna know about this girl."

"Deal."

———

Tank scanned the display case. "I can't make up my mind. This one...or this princess cut over here." He pointed to the rings.

Kasper had been silently searching for the perfect ring himself. He found it fifteen minutes ago. All there was left to do was ask his best friend for his blessing. Sure, he was okay with their relationship, but they'd only been together for a few weeks this time. Not only that, asking Tank would be as close as he could get to asking her father. His throat suddenly felt like the Sahara Desert.

"Paxton." He swallowed the lump in his throat.

Tank turned his head slowly. So fucking slow it was like the world was in slow motion. His eyebrow quirked up, clearly his way of asking a question. His hands stayed braced on the glass counter. He waited.

"Mr. S was like a father to me, more than my own was. You know that. I want to honor him and hope he's proud of the man I'm becoming. I couldn't do it without your sister. She's...she's fuckin' everything. I want to marry her. I want to have a small gaggle of kids with her, if that's what she wants. I know you might think it's too fast..." he pushed on quickly before Tank could respond. "But I've loved her as far back as I can remember. Since fucking John picked her up to take her to the movies the first time —even longer." He sighed, rubbing the back of his neck.

"Knowing you, you already picked out a ring too," he scoffed.

Kasper pointed. Tank's gaze followed his finger. Tank eyed him quizzically. He returned his look with a smile.

"I can't believe you picked a ring before me. Bullshit. That's what that is." Shaking his head, he pulled Kasper into a hug. "Just be good to her."

———

Krysta came in while he paced the master bedroom, rehearsing what he was going to say to her tonight over dinner.

"Who are you talking to?" She cocked her head to the side slightly.

She looked stunning in a pair of yoga pants and sports bra that zipped up the front. He wanted to pull it down with his teeth. Her skin glowed. Placing her hands on her hips, she waited for an answer. He wanted an answer too. He slipped his hand in his pocket, gripped the small velvet box. No, he had a plan. He would take her to their spot. She would like that.

"Kass, you're making me nervous. Say something."

He took a deep breath, dropping down to one knee in front of her. He reached for her hand, but she snatched it away.

"You ass-face," she screamed. "What the hell are you doing?"

He sighed, exasperated. This wasn't the reaction he was expecting. She never made things easy. "What does it look like I'm doing?"

"And you think this is the time to do this? While I'm a hot and sweaty mess?"

"I think anytime I want to tell the most amazing woman in the world that I love her and want to spend my every fucking tomorrow with her is the right time. I happen to like you when you're a hot, sweaty mess."

This time he grabbed her hand with a playful sneer. He retrieved the red velvet box from his pocket, holding it out as an offering, not yet lifting the lid. Now that he was here before her, nerves snaked up his spine. He was completely nontraditional in his choice of engagement rings. What if she didn't like it? What if she wanted some huge diamond solitaire? The geometric moss agate stone set in a gold band with small diamonds on each side was extraordinary. He had been drawn to the ring because it was different and intriguing and beautiful, just like the woman who would, hopefully, wear it. He swallowed his nerves down.

"Krys, it's no secret I've made mistakes. I can't promise I won't in the future. We'll piss each other off and fight and make up and live. Live this life together. I promise I won't stop working to be a man you can be proud to call your husband. I won't stop working to be the best father I can be when that time comes. And I want it to come soon. I can promise I won't stop choosing *you*. I've never loved another woman. I know I never will. You're it for me. My favorite person. My north star. Please, make me the happiest son of a bitch on earth." He let her hand go, lifting the lid on the little box. She gasped. "Marry me?"

"On one condition…"

He quirked an eyebrow, tilting his head. His woman never made things easy.

"Don't ever let me catch you wearing a man bun again." A cheeky grin lit her face up and she wiggled her ring finger.

Kasper slid the ring onto it, kissing the top of her hand,

then her forehead before capturing her perfect lips. He swooped her up, tossing her on the bed. Pulling his shirt from his body, he gave her a mischievous grin. "Now, Future Mrs. Guttenmuth, how about we get started on those rug rats?"

EPILOGUE: ONE

KRYSTA

KRYSTA STOOD in front of the full-length mirror, smoothing her hands down her dress. Turning side to side, she studied her appearance. Her ring sparkled in the reflection.

"You look beautiful." Sloane startled her.

Turning to face the woman she considered a sister in every way besides blood, she gushed, "Me? Look at you. Max is going to be beside himself."

Sloane's ivory dress was nothing short of perfection on her. The lace corset bodice gave the illusion it was sheer. Three-dimensional floral lace appliques adorned the bodice, cascading down to the bottom of the gown. The wide hemline swished when she walked. Krysta thought the dress was gorgeous on its own, but once Sloane slipped the detachable bishop sleeves on, she looked like a fantasy. Max was seriously going to lose his shit.

Krysta, Cori, and Marabella wore A-line off the shoulder asymmetrical dresses in hunter green, with a beaded waistline. The airy chiffon would hide the small bump she was currently rocking. It had only taken two months for Kasper to make good on his promise on rug rats. She was four months along now.

"Are you ready?" Marabella asked, handing the bridal bouquet to her cousin.

"I am." She took the flowers, a dozen white roses, and called to her daughter. "Mia, baby, time to walk to daddy."

Mia set down the tablet she was watching. The ivory tooling pooled up around her little hips as she slid off the chair. They lined up outside, just beyond view of any of the guests. They emerged from the tree line one by one as an instrumental version of Elvis Presley's *Can't Help Falling in Love* played through the speakers surrounding the pond in the clearing behind Max and Sloane's house.

Lights twinkled everywhere like fireflies—above their heads, mason jars on tables, and lanterns along the aisle they would walk. It was a fairytale. The guests all watched, eager to see the bride as Cori started walking toward the makeshift altar the guys made. It was also adorned with artificial vines, flowers, and lights. Marabella followed a few steps behind her. Krysta leaned down to Mia to whisper to her.

"Okay, little lady. When I get to that chair," she pointed, "you come follow me until you find your daddy. Got it?"

"Yup." She nodded enthusiastically.

Krysta didn't think she would remember, but that was okay. She glanced over her shoulder to watch a pair of hands wave Mia to go. Krysta met her husband's heated stare as she took her place in front of Marabella. He covered his heart with his left hand. She would never get tired of the jolt of pride she got when she glimpsed his black tungsten wedding band.

Mia squealed, "Daddy!" running the rest of the way to

Max. The love he had for his daughter was evident in his smile. He caught her as she leapt into his arms. He swung her around, kissing her forehead. "Go sit with Gramma." He pointed to his mom in the front row.

The music changed. The opening notes of *Crystal* played as Sloane stepped into the open. Soft murmurs from the guests didn't distract Max one iota. His stare was fixed, his mouth slightly agape as he waited for Sloane to stand by his side. Sloane smiled, matching tears in her eyes. She kissed her father before turning to Max. The emotions, the love these two had for each other was undeniable. It was a physical thing, even a blind man could recognize it in the way the air shifted around them.

The song was about finding love. They had. So had she. So had Paxton and Foster. She had a sneaky suspicion Benji might have too, that is if the curvy blonde sitting next to him was what it looked like.

She was pulled from her thoughts as the pastor raised his voice in celebration. "I now pronounce you husband and wife. You may kiss your bride, Maxwell." And kiss her he did.

The reception was a blast. The dancing, the food, the company. The food. Pregnancy made her want to stuff her face with everything. Kasper stalked across the yard to her. He had that predatory look in his eyes again. Usually, she ended up naked not soon after. Wrapping his strong arms around her, he kissed her forehead, his lips lingering a moment.

"Hey there, wife."

"You look like you're up to no good."

"Who me?" He feigned innocence. "Dance with me."

"You wanna do the Cha Cha shuffle?" she asked

incredulously, eyes sweeping over the dance floor at the crowd as they clapped, laughing with each other.

"Absofuckinlutely not," he supplied her with a repulsed look. "I asked the DJ to play something next. We may not have had a reception, but I still want my first dance."

Her heart skipped a beat as it always did when he did little things to show he cared. It wasn't just words with him. It was everything. The DJ turned down the music to speak.

"Ladies and gentlemen, seems we have another newly minted married couple out here. They still haven't had their first dance. Kasper has picked out a special one for his new bride. Come on out here." He waved. "Got a little *Never Stop* by SafetySuit for ya."

Kasper twirled her onto the wooden dance floor. She wrapped her arms around him as he swayed them back and forth. The words melting her heart. "I love you, Krysta Guttenmuth. Until my dying breath."

"I love you more. More than any argument. More than any hardship we may face. More than anything."

The song ended, Kasper dipped her over his arm, sealing his lips over hers.

EPILOGUE: TWO

KASPER

6 Years Later...

"LITTLE DUDE," Kasper yelled, throwing his hands in the air in frustration. He didn't think his life could get better after marrying the love of his life. Then they had Remington. Life was crazy and beautiful, and he wouldn't trade a single second of it. "What did I tell you about pushing your sister?"

"To not to," their son, Waylon, answered sheepishly, twiddling his fingers.

"That's right. We don't hit girls," he scolded.

"But...but...even if, what if she told me I stink?" His eyes widened like dinner plates with the force of his words.

Tank laughed heartily while wrapping an arm around Cori. "Do you stink?"

"No. It's not funny, Uncle Pax," the four-year-old cried out in frustration.

"Yeah, Uncle Pax." Max hid a smile behind his beer bottle.

Kasper crouched down to meet his son's eyes. "Even if she tells you that you stink. We don't hurt girls. Ever. Go on. Go find Remi and play. I think he's in the bounce house."

"M'kay, Dad."

"Little Mama," he called after Waylon's twin sister, Ruby. She was huddled in deep conversation with Julianna, Tank's daughter. At least as deep as one could expect from four-year-olds. She barely spared him a glance.

"Sorry," she hollered.

Krysta smiled as she approached the group with Trevor on her right hip. She looked exhausted. Putting together a birthday party for Remington on top of everything else she did daily wasn't easy. He'd have to give her a foot massage tonight after all the kids were in bed. She glowed though, and he swore he fell in love with her more each time he laid eyes on her. Her hair was swept up in a messy bun, which was a little hypocritical since he couldn't wear one, but a deal was a deal.

"That girl," he motioned to Ruby, "she's your guts."

"One of them needed to be. Three miniature versions of you is more than this world can handle."

"Gutter, can you please keep your mitts off my baby sister?"

Krysta rubbed her swollen belly with her left hand, laughing. She was due in three weeks. He couldn't wait to hold that precious baby girl in his arms. They'd wasted no time in building their family. They were about to be a family of seven. He promised her when he proposed, he would give her as many kids as she wanted. He'd kept every promise, he wasn't about to start breaking any now.

"Me? Why am I blamed? Your sister is insatiable. I'm

the one getting deliciously violated whenever the urge strikes her."

"Aww, poor baby." Foster rolled his eyes.

Kasper's attention was drawn to the swing set. Remington pushed Waylon next to where Seth pushed his sister Maryanne. Marabella had some complications with the delivery of Maryanne. They decided if they wanted more kids in the future there were plenty of children out there that needed a loving family.

Sloane and Max were comfortable with Mia and Colton and their three dogs. Fear Inc. had been doing well. They took less cases of infidelity and more cases working with the families of missing persons. They all felt they were actually making a difference now.

"Can you believe he's six already?" Krysta wrapped her arm around him. He ruffled Trevor's mop of hair.

"No. Time is moving too quickly. I lost so many years —" She pressed a finger to his lips, silencing him.

"The past is the past."

"You're right."

"I usually am." She grinned.

"Ha," he scoffed. "You wish."

"Speaking of the past, I think there's going to be another addition to the family."

"No shit, have you seen this thing?" he asked, rubbing her belly.

Playfully she slapped his arm. "Paxton has put his hand on Cori's stomach four times in the last hour. I don't even think he realizes it."

"I hope it's a boy. Julianna is just like Doc. He doesn't deserve that. I hope he has a hellraiser just like he was."

"You do know girls can be hellraisers too, right?"

"Of course."

"Good, because we might have one."

"Ruby's a good girl...mostly." He laughed. "Well, twenty-five percent of the time. Maybe a little less."

"Not Ruby." Krysta looked down. The front of her shorts sported a large wet spot. She set Trevor down and rubbed her belly.

"Shit, did she kick your bladder again?"

"No, she broke my water."

"Are you fucking serious?"

She glared at him as if he were a moron and this wasn't her fifth kid. Yeah, he could be dumb sometimes. He kissed her hard on the mouth. It was time.

"Hot damn," he whooped. "We're having a baby!"

"Cat's been outta the bag for a while now, dipshit," Tank called out. Kasper gave his brother-in-law the finger. Everyone laughed. The kids continued to run and play between both yards since they still lived next door to Tank and Cori. They bought Cori's house after they eloped.

"As in now," Krysta replied.

Marabella waved them to go. "We've got the kids. Don't worry about a thing."

"We'll call the grandparents," Max added.

He meant all of them. They were a family. Family not only looked out for their own, but they pitched in when needed and celebrated milestones as often as possible. Cori ran into the house to get the hospital bag Krysta had packed just last week, while Tank started the car. Kasper placed his hand on the small of her back.

"Let's go, Kitten." He beamed at her. "We're burnin' daylight."

The End

BEFORE YOU GO...

If you enjoyed my book please take a quick second to leave a short review on Amazon. These reviews help me as an author be found by other amazing readers like you.

Thank you so much! :)

ABOUT THE AUTHOR

Melinda Valentine was born in upstate New York. Being the youngest of four children (and the only girl) made it easy for her to turn to books as companions. As a young child, she was whisked away to Baltimore, Maryland and spent her youth reading books such as *Nancy Drew*, *The Chronicles of Narnia*, and *The Little House on the Prairie* saga.

However, it wasn't until she was twelve years old that she read a book (Stephen King's *IT*) that made her realize that someday, she would herself become a writer. After that, her first (horrible) manuscript came to life, and at thirteen she had received her very first rejection letter. Heartbroken, she continued to read even more to learn about the craft of writing.

Today Melinda calls West Virginia home, with her swoon-worthy husband, hilarious children, and three crazy puppies of all ages. She hopes her readers fall in love with her characters as much as she has.

Website:
http://www.melindavalentine.com/

www.ingramcontent.com/pod-product-compliance
Lightning Source LLC
Chambersburg PA
CBHW020912180626
46816CB00007BA/2370